ROOKED

CHAPTER 1

Raising her dollar store flute to toast the wasted mass of acquaintances in front of her, Ara Hopkins gulped down cheap champagne, plastered on her most believable smile, and began making her way through the New Year's hopefuls and falling confetti.

Ara felt about New Year's Eve the way most people felt about riding a crowded subway car on a hot New York City day. Claustrophobic. Fighting crowds for enough oxygen to avoid the slow burning pain of suffocation was not her ideal. But she was good at faking it, at least; she'd taught herself how to come out on top long ago. It was basic survival of the fittest—or the most f'ed up. Whether the elite or the sludge of humanity won at life was a classic game of chess known all too well to its occupants.

The best part about the city, though, was that it was forgiving at its core, allowing you to be whoever you wanted the next day, no matter what troll you had resembled the night before. Anything could be chalked up to evolution of character.

Still, Ara hated the pressure of New Year's Eve and its "New Year, New Me" hashtags. The pathetic promises partygoers made to themselves, conveniently disguised as elaborate, imitative resolutions. The sparkling two-thousand-whatever party favors people felt forced to wear. It also could be the holiday's ability to label you a pathetic loser for lacking a midnight kiss. New Year's Eve topped the worst days to be single charts, second only to Valentine's Day, the most messed up holiday of the year. What a fresh way to kick off the much-hated hashtags. Hashtag screw brunch, hashtag I'd rather sleep in, hashtag let's stop being fake and acting like we like each other. The hipster resolutioners were the best example. Their paleo, cross fitting, Namaste kicks often ending in despairing, binge-eating mutilations. *Damn,* Ara thought, *we millennials can be so dull.*

She promised herself never to be so pathetic. Not for a second did she dream of a social media certified existence. As if nothing in this life actually happened unless it was confirmed through a snappy Instagram post, complete with a clever caption, so loads of double-tapping 'friends' could show their stamp of approval.

Ara Hopkins seemed normal though, by all millennial standards. It was on the inside where she despised it all. But lately, she felt like she'd reached a tipping point of sorts, becoming increasingly unsatisfied with her repetitive, yet chaotic life and now having to 'make something of herself' in a down economy that despised her generation. What about the bastard baby boomers who seemed to repeatedly screw the generation and the country that would eventually need to care for them? And they said millennials were self-absorbed.

She needed a plan, and not having one twisted her stomach in knots. How could she be expected to sit back and hope all the plays fell in her favor? Despite the numerous three a.m. insomnia-induced self-help Google searches and soothing mantras that promised her the ability to become as peaceful as Buddha himself, Ara enjoyed being in control and loved nothing more than a good, solid strategy for this game called life. Her therapist, Dr. Dan, had a name for it, said it was a fear of imperfection. Ara could only wonder, who wouldn't want a perfect life?

For as long as she could remember, she had been mapping out her future. Get in to a good college; meet the perfect guy, preferably from a financially comfortable family; have a successful career; and live happily ever after. But little by little, one disappointing casual hook up after another, she began to realize her perfect plan was dangerously off track. The education part was easy, but finding Prince Charming in a packed college bar when there was always a younger, drunker, and more promiscuous bandeau-wearing girl waiting on deck, was not quite the same. Maybe she should have picked a school where the female-to-male ratio was less than four to one.

And there was always Raina.

Raina Martin, queen of said millennials—who somehow managed to defend the title of Ara's "stepsister and best friend"—was sloppily kissing a guy named James on their newly-purchased Craigslist love seat. A familiar occurrence: Raina preoccupied in casual lust while Ara awkwardly pretended not to notice getting ditched for the night.

After spending four years as roommates, mostly due to their parents' encouragement, Ara was convinced that Raina's greatest aphrodisiac was seducing any guy with a pulse away from her—despite Raina repeatedly claiming her innocence in situations where she just happened to end up in bed with one of Ara's crushes. Fact being, that girl desperately needed male attention. It never seemed to matter that

4

when a hook up didn't call her again, she would find herself with her head in the toilet and a mascara-stained face, slurring that all guys were pigs. And it definitely never seemed to register that Ara was the only one rubbing her back at three a.m. after a night of Cuervo. Raina wanted love, and idiotically thought she found it in every beer-soaked weekend hot spot.

Raina was also the reason she and Ara were hosting this party, despite Ara's hatred of the holiday. Year after year, Raina would insist they host their annual soiree, with pinky promises that the party would be better than the last. But come every January first, over a hangover-friendly meal on a sticky table that still needed to be wiped clean with Clorox, they swore that they would never host again.

But Raina always got her way. Manipulation was her strongest, and most fruitful asset. Like a smooth politician, she knew how to work a room, and she could also convince even the toughest of critics that casual sex was always a good thing.

"Ara! Come meet James's friend." Raina had come up for air and was forcing her way through the other inebriated twenty-somethings. "He's super hot! And I think he's a lawyer!"

Annoyed, Ara pushed through the crowd, brushing past Lane, a new addition to the group she didn't quite know yet, and was met with a stunning pair of sharp blue eyes, possibly the brightest she had ever seen. "James's friend," who she recognized as a prominent New York congressman's son, raised his hand, loosely gripping hers, and flashed a perfect Calvin Klein smile. Standing over her at six foot two, Ara could already tell she would fit perfectly into the nook between his shoulder and arm, her favorite spot of the male anatomy.

"Brad Bugia, law student, not lawyer," said the now-named object of Ara's attention.

"Ara Hopkins."

This was her big play in life, she had finally won her game.

Or so she'd thought.

Five years and one month later, Ara found herself frozen with shock, staring down at Brad's lifeless body on the floor of their waterfront apartment in Newport, New Jersey.

It was like something out of a clumsy, cheesy horror movie, not reality. Red pools of blood filled any available crevice on their wood floor. Ara tried to scream but the words were lodged somewhere painfully deep in the pit of her stomach, a dreadful place she hadn't believed existed until that exact moment. Where the pain was, unrecognizable to a 90's raised, upper class, woman as herself.

She collapsed on top of him. Despite all logic telling her she needed to call 911 and get help, the bullet hole in his chest made it clear there was nothing anyone could do. She stared at the youthful, chiseled features, slowly turning stone gray as his blood stopped warming him. His face veiled in an ominous look of untimely death. She finally let out an anguished cry for their life together, from the moment they'd met to the overbearing one rushing at her from every corner of the room.

Their night played out in her head. Together for five years, married for two of them, she loved how they still dated. The dinner tonight had been at Del Posto's in Chelsea near the Highline. They'd filled themselves with Italian delicacies and a bottle of overpriced red wine Brad had been happy to purchase off a back page of the extensive, wine list, even springing for a modern tiramisu despite not usually being the dessert ordering types.

"We're moving up! No more by the glass table red for us," Brad had said as they'd coyly clicked their glasses, her taking the tiniest of sips. She could tell he'd already had a drink or two after work, and she knew that he'd pour for himself with a heavy hand tonight, oblivious to the fact she was barely sipping her alcohol.

A flirtatious car ride home across the river to their Newport apartment had mimicked the most passionate ride of a one-night stand. Lip-locked, with eager hands exploring each other between disapproving glances in the rear-view mirror from the Uber driver. Then, despite her protests, Brad telling her to wait in the lobby for ten minutes before coming up to the apartment. Explaining quickly as he exited the car that he had a surprise planned for them and needed time to set it up. Brad knew Ara hated surprises more than any of the other things that irked her: the dentist, crowded trains on hot days, etc. Being surprised topped her list. Instead of rousing excitement in her like they were supposed to, surprises usually left Ara uneasy and anxious about having the correct reaction the surpriser expected.

But not Brad. Brad *loved* surprises and every bit of the rush of excitement that came with them. An adrenaline junkie and life-on-the-edge kind of guy, every aspect of Brad's life was a game for him just waiting to be played. He'd been that way since birth: if Ara had heard the tale of his twenty-three minute, exhilarating journey into this world once, she'd heard it a million times. His mother had practically delivered him through her '80s-era Madonna style floral leggings while hospital staff had frantically tried to get her situated in a room.

"Always the wild card!" Brad's mother would say as his father, a pillar in the New York Democratic party and a current congressman, would brag how he knew since that moment that his only son would be destined for great things.

Tonight, Brad had untangled himself from Ara's hold and waltzed to the elevator, giving her one last wink before the bronze doors closed in front of him like Broadway curtains following a show's final scenes. He and his magic were gone.

Left feeling anxious and cold in the February air, Ara followed far enough behind him so that he wouldn't turn around. After entering the building they'd called home for four years, she decided to take the stairs to their seventh-floor apartment. The hike up the dark, rear staircase would probably take the exact amount of time Brad requested her wait. This wasn't the first time she'd dragged herself up the stairs. It was something of a stress reliever when something was on her mind, and she'd done the exact same thing many times in the weeks prior. And, of course, in the early days when she'd wanted the perfect peach emoji-worthy ass for their honeymoon.

Now here she was. Here they were. Their textbook romance and pleasant life, seemingly created just for the two of them, radically cut short, stripped from existence. Their safe, cozy, love-filled home violated. *Why did this have to happen here?*

"Ma'am, step away from the body!" Ara looked up and saw three police officers standing in her doorway. Of course, one of her neighbors would have called 911 after hearing gunshots. This neighborhood prided itself on both its security, and its residents' involvement in the community. Frozen from a blend of shock and fear, she could do nothing but stare blankly at the officers and defensively pull Brad in closer to her.

"Ma'am." The uniformed men started toward her. Slow at first, as if she was a rabid animal that could pounce at any moment, then more forcefully, pulling her away from Brad, allowing his lifeless body to slump back to the floor with a thud. Ara started screaming and kicking, desperately trying to fight off the men taking her away from him. Tears streaked her once perfectly contoured face as another officer rushed toward her. Knowing that acting reckless in a situation like this would get her nowhere, she submitted to the officers, collecting herself to avoid being physically subdued.

"Ma'am, you need to calm down and tell us what happened here," the tallest of the growing group of law enforcement said, just inches from her face—close enough for her to smell the charred Dunkin Donuts coffee from the corner shop. "We can't help you if you don't work with us," he said, letting loose another whiff of rancid caramel coffee, flipping her stomach.

All of her words seemed lodged in her throat.

"I don't know, I just came in and . . . Please help him," she said as the lead detective moved back and stared hard into Ara's fear-filled eyes as she struggled to put a coherent sentence together.

"Your husband is dead," he said. "And since you are the only one here, it looks to me like you might know something about that."

The room began to spin. The intricately decorated walls that she and Brad had spent hours perfecting reeled uncontrollably around her.

Numbness ran from the tips of her fingers straight down her spine. And this time, she vomited for real.

The officers stopped trying to question her and pulled Ara to a chair in the back corner of the room. She sat there for what felt like hours as the forensics team began combing through her living room, taking bits and pieces of her life away in evidence bags. When Lane walked in, she was never happier to see him. Brad's life-long friend—almost a brother to him—and a brother to the boys in blue. A detective in neighboring Manhattan, she knew it was hard for him to keep his composure as he stepped past his best friend to comfort her.

Over the past five years, the two had become quite close, though Lane had been distant as of late.

Ara jumped from the seat and ran to his arms. Lane's arms wrapped comfortingly around her, and after lingering in a defeated hug, Ara pulled away, as he brushed the free strands of hair from her face.

"Ara! Are you OK, what happened? I rushed here as soon as I heard over the radio, somehow the news already got to the city."

"I just came in and found him like this. It finally killed him, it freakin' killed him, Lane," Ara said, her mind racing through all that has happened in the last few weeks.

"What? Who killed Brad, Ara? You aren't making any sense." Lane stared back, searching for an answer she was not able to give. Not knowing what to say, all she could do was shake her head, one hand covering her mouth.

"The detectives will figure this all out, Ara. Don't you worry— we'll get this all figured out."

She let her head slump to his chest and took in her first deep breath since the car ride home.

CHAPTER 2

He yearned for moments like this. Watching Ara as she meandered her way through everyday existence breathed life into his otherwise useless soul. No slut from the downtown bars could get him going like she could. He liked to think she knew he was watching, flirting with him from afar, and that they were playing a private game, just the two of them. But he knew the truth. He was a lot of things but he wasn't a fool, that's for damn sure.

He didn't mind being on the outside looking in—that's what he told himself, at least. And he had tried to give it all up—he really had. He straightened, looked at himself in the mirror, and promised he would give up on her for good, let her move on…and so would he. But the depression and withdrawal that came with quitting her cold turkey was too much to bear. This was the better resolution to his addiction. This way, he could have her all to himself.

A town car pulled to the curb outside Del Posto's and the pair got in. Him first, then her. She'd paused, looking back like she'd known he was there, before lowering herself into the car.

"Not tonight, you desperate bastard," he'd said aloud to himself. "Go the hell home."

But his cravings won, and the two black cars, theirs and his, waltzed their way through the center of the universe and back through the tunnel to New Jersey.

CHAPTER 3

Ara's fear-shaken legs, still exposed in her bloodied Donna Karen dress, clung to the cold metallic chairs. *They must keep it cold on purpose*, she thought, *to make you as miserable as possible.* Her head propped on her forearm, Ara's eyes lingered on the interrogation room table. Inches away, the vapors from her mouth turned to fog as she allowed herself to shallowly inhale and exhale.

"Mrs. Bugia, you are going to have to start being honest with us. The gun that was most likely used in the murder was registered to you and your husband," Detective Maro, the smaller but more experienced of the two said. "What's a successful, good-looking couple like you two doing with a nine-millimeter handgun?"

Ara ignored him and continued to watch the vapors as they danced disfigured shapes across the shiny surface. Appearing and then disappearing. Gone almost as soon as they came. Just like her now dead husband. Never one to be considered 'clutch' in a high stress situation, Ara could feel the heat of an anxiety attack flood her face.

"Mrs. Bugia?" The frustration in the detective's voice was becoming more and more evident. Ara didn't care. To her it was nothing more than noise. Meaningless, white noise.

"She already told you everything she knows," Lane interjected. He was playing a balancing act between friend and detective, and thanks to Lane's smooth yet persistent demeanor and a little thing called professional courtesy, the investigating officers had allowed him to remain in the room while they interrogated Ara. "Brad wanted protection, he had gotten into some matters with clients that he wasn't comfortable with. I went with him and helped pick out the gun and showed both Ara and him how to use it."

"You saying this is a suicide, Bene?" Ameno, the younger detective, chirped.

"I'm saying that when she got off that elevator, she found him shot dead on the floor." Lane stared desperately at Ara, as if looking for any hint of emotion that would validate her story to the skeptical, ready-to-pounce, detectives.

But instead all she said was, "It's Hopkins. Ara Hopkins. I never changed my last name when we got married."

The stares sharpened around her as one detective took note of the comment on his legal pad and the other one shook his head, obviously choosing to disregard her comment. "Fine, Bene, you're saying the victim wants to surprise her, so she waits in the car, comes up to the apartment a few minutes after. The problem is she's not on the security tape and is covered in his blood. Her goddamn bloody fingerprints are all over him and the apartment. If she waited in the lobby, she would be on that tape."

Lane continued to dispute the detective's allegations as Ara slipped off into another haze. Her head felt heavy and was weighing her down, her neck suddenly not strong enough to hold it up.

Resting her face on her forearms, she allowed the detectives to argue for another minute or so before finally saying, "I took the stairs. Didn't you see that on the tape?" Three sets of eyes now focused directly on her. "I was nervous about waiting in the car, and it was freezing out, so I decided to take the stairs."

Ara had watched enough crime shows to know they were analyzing her every word, judging the authenticity of her emotions and the tears that fell from her eyes. She always wondered why the of-course-suspected spouse wouldn't think to act a certain way, or at least be aware that the detectives were clearly scrutinizing him or her. But now she knew. Her husband was dead, and her life was changed forever. She couldn't care less what this high-school-quarterback-who-never-left-his-hometown detective thought of her.

Lane repeated, "She took the stairs, Maro. See? Problem solved." Lane seemed satisfied with the answer, and Ara hoped the others would be, too.

Detective Maro, the obvious bad cop, pushed back his chair and chuckled, and pointed obnoxiously at Ara's feet.

"You expect us to believe that you hiked up seven flights of stairs in those heels? What are they four, five inches?" His chair screeched as he dragged it back in, sending a shiver straight down Ara's spine.

Yes, I do expect you to believe that. Walking up the stairs had given her plenty of time to get herself together for whatever Brad wanted. Tonight, more than ever, she'd needed the time to compose herself.

Lane jumped to her defense, the conversation getting more and more heated. "I'm sure her phone's health app could prove this, Maro." The testosterone filling the room as the men squared off was too much for her. Who were they to analyze her every move? Tonight was supposed to have been nothing more than an enjoyable date night for her and her husband. She should be asleep right now, in the deep rest that only came after a perfectly-timed orgasm. Instead, here she was with three douchebags trying to figure out who'd broken into her house and shot her husband in cold blood. She'd had enough.

"I don't like surprises. Brad knows that. I hate them. But he didn't care tonight and wanted to surprise me anyway," she said, pausing for a moment. *And now he's dead. How is that for a surprise?* She shook her head at the thought and lowered her voice. "I needed a little time to relax. I've taken the stairs plenty of times. Whoever did this, it wasn't me."

The men stopped their bickering—maybe it was the shock of hearing her speak after being so silent. "We'll go back to the tape, Ms. Hopkins, look again for any other potential suspects." She hardly heard the detective as her mind drifted to the day Brad proposed.

She was probably the only woman in the world who'd been pinched with anger instead of joy the moment after the proposal, because her fiancé-to-be had gotten away with surprising her in the dimly-lit upstate New York restaurant. Cozy, with a large booming fireplace and snow trickling outside the window, many women would have killed for an intimate, surprise proposal like the one Brad planned. *This stuff excites people, makes them happy,* she'd thought as she responded "Yes" to Brad's perfectly pitched proposition. Luckily, as usual, Brad had been unfazed, used to her idiosyncrasies by then. He'd scooped her up in his arms and posed for the photo session he planned with their waiter to capture the moment. *He really thought of everything.* Ara clumsily went through the motions of ecstatic wife-to-be while Brad had scrolled through his contacts informing everyone, family and friends, of what just happened. Ara didn't send a single text at first, though she would have to tell Raina eventually. The thought of her mother finding out from an overly hashtagged post to Raina's Instagram was more thrilling than the fact that she was now engaged to one of New York's most eligible bachelors. As expected, her mother numbed herself with Valium and rosé until Ara called a few days after she and Brad returned to the city.

She recalled feeling overwhelmed at the thought of spending the rest of their lives together. If only she'd known then that it would only be a few more short years, and that the promise of 'forever' was far less permanent than she'd thought. They would never have children or go to Bora Bora like they planned. All the jokes they'd shared about growing old and gray together were now fictional. Brad would never grow old. He would never be gray. He would forever be the thirty-two-year-old up-and-comer who *really could have been something*. People would mourn him, shocked by the travesty of such a young talent snuffed out— only to move on to the next big life event after they socially shared their condolences. Once a year she'd receive sympathetic anniversary messages laced with the standard "he's in a better place" and "he would want you to be happy," only to be forgotten again until the next tragically marked year since his death. But her life would be forever tarnished. She would never have the opportunity to return to normal. Her normalcy had bled out on their American Cherry wood floors.

"I think we're done here for today. Ara has been through a lot." Lane put his hands on her shoulders possessively, staring down the other detectives who stared right back, the "we're the law" attitude impossible to ignore.

"Sure, Detective Bene. But first we need that dress. And her pretty little shoes, too," said Maro, snickering to his partner.

Standing, Lane said, "Come on, Ara, let's get this over with."

"Before you go, Bene, one more question. How'd you get to the scene so fast?" Detective Ameno asked.

"Heard it over the radio," Lane said as he continued toward the door.

Ameno put his arm up, blocking them from exiting, "All the way across the river?"

"A New York congressman's only son was shot in Jersey, guess the news traveled fast. Excuse us."

Ameno dropped his arm and Ara unhesitatingly let Lane lead her out of the interrogation room and down the short hallway to the closet-sized area where her clothes would be collected as evidence.

Afterwards, feeling like a criminal in the scrub-like replacement clothes provided, Ara walked toward the exit as Maro reappeared in the doorway. Scowling, she knew he was going in for a *Law and Order*-like punch line to keep viewers hinged to the TV through the commercial break.

"One more question, Ms. Hopkins. Did you hear it? The gunshot?"

He sure is proud of himself for that one, she thought, but before she could answer, a commotion distracted everyone: Raina, forcing her way through security. Some guy Ara didn't recognize retreated near the entrance of the police station, clearly regretting his decision to accompany Raina here that evening. Ara smiled slightly at the thought of this poor soul telling his friends the one-night stand horror story over a craft beer at some Hoboken bro bar. Getting interrupted mid-hookup only to be dragged to the police station by a girl he barely knew to rescue her stepsister that he definitely didn't know. Barstool humor at its finest. They'd all laugh and high-five away the pain that the night's event had brought to her.

"Ara!" Raina raced toward her, pushing past the security guard. As always, she looked flawless, if a little over the top, complete with full makeup, winged eyeliner, and pouty lips. Ara wondered if Raina was hoping she would be photographed leaving the police station.

"Oh my God, Ara! Oh my God. Brad is dead? All I heard at first was that someone was shot, I'm so happy you're all right," Raina sobbed as she threw her arms around Ara and squeezed her obnoxiously tight. Two things Raina loved: invading personal space and soap opera-like dramatics. Ara couldn't help but notice Raina seemed shocked that it was Brad, not her, who had been killed.

Still, Ara allowed Raina to hold her. Despite all the damning sides of their relationship, they both, on the surface, always supported each other. Since their first introduction on a visit to the college the two would eventually attend, the girls knew their parents would expect them to become the best of friends. It was a year later, over warm beers from a keg at the Rugby House, that they drunkenly promised to make their friendship work, deciding it was better to have an ally in their now joined family than an enemy. But Ara knew that it was times like these that tested friendships, and theirs was often tenuous.

"Lane, please tell me you didn't let them rough her up. If it's anything like the ID channel, they'll have her admitting to murder and in jail rooming with a trophy wife, turned soon to be divorcee, turned convicted murderer by morning!"

"Sshh! Raina, watch it before they make you the state's star witness against her with that mouth of yours." Lane was sounding more and more frustrated by the minute. His fuse was normally quite short with Raina, and tonight it seemed practically nonexistent.

As Lane and Raina argued over Ara's sleeping arrangements, Ara turned back to Detective Maro, who lingered like a snake in the grass down the hall. It was not her fault Brad was dead. And she refused to leave with anyone, especially the detective, thinking that it was.

With her most confident, no-nonsense stare, Ara said, "No, Detective. I did not hear the shot. I told you, I was in the stairwell."

CHAPTER 4

Lane couldn't pull his eyes away from Ara. Sitting next to him, watching her own breath form shapes on the interrogation room table. Despite her current circumstances, she still looked perfect to him. Her hair brushed casually over her shoulder, and her face, though flooded with streams of tears, was still as beautiful as the first day he'd laid eyes on her.

He remembered the New Year's party like it was yesterday: Ara standing across the room, awkwardly sipping her champagne, clearly uncomfortable being alone at midnight. He didn't know who she was, but had wondered how a woman who looked like that could seem unconscious of the bewitching effect she was having on him. Didn't she know she was beautiful?

With a ping of nervousness, he'd scanned the room while the other partygoers hardly took notice. Brad was casually flirting with a group of girls in body-hugging dresses and platform heels. Unlike the women gripping Brad's attention, Ara wore a classic black dress with subtle sparkling appliqués trickling down the mid-length sleeves, her hair pulled back softly to one side. She was exquisite. And he had to meet her, find out who she was with. Who was he kidding, he had to find out everything about her. His mind had raced as he'd wondered what her favorite color was and if she preferred pancakes or French toast on cozy Sunday mornings. He was sure she would laugh at his jokes, and probably loved reading on the beach.

"Three, two, one. Happy New Year!"

Lane had pushed off the wall and grabbed a second glass of champagne. He started toward the center of the room, weaving between the kissing lovers and bitter loners, gawking at the ridiculous display of affection. He had to save her. Cliché as it was, she was too perfect to be left alone at midnight.

But Raina had gotten in the way of what could have been.

"Ara!" He'd learned her name when Raina had shouted it. "Meet James's friend. I think he's a lawyer!" Lane tried again to move himself through the crowd but Ara brushed past him, so close he could smell her perfume. Or her shampoo. Whatever it was, it was delicious.

Crushed by his bad timing as he watched Ara meet Brad, Lane retreated to the wall, knowing things would never be the same. Cursing Raina for getting in his way.

Now here, in this room, Lane wanted to believe Ara was innocent and that she could never kill Brad. Ara wouldn't hurt a fly. She was kind and compassionate, a class all to her own. It was for that reason he stayed away over the past few years. He blamed his job with its long hours and tempting overtime, but truth be told, Lane simply couldn't bear to be around Ara if she was Brad's wife. It was a hopeless battle between his desire for her and his loyalty to Brad, his childhood friend of almost thirty years. It was too hard to give up on her and the last thing he needed was Brad to be suspicious. They were best friends. Who just so happened to be attracted to the same woman. An age-old love triangle.

It wasn't the first time Lane fantasized about a way he and Ara could be together, when he would have a chance to show how he felt. He would have never wanted Brad dead, but now that he was, this could be his time. Ara, alone and vulnerable. Surely she would need someone to comfort her, take care of her, and he could offer her something Brad never could—he would love her only.

CHAPTER 5

The cheap fabric that covered Raina's couch scratched at Ara's skin. Sleep was barely there even though she was heavily sedated by a cocktail of Ambien and antidepressants and shaking herself awake seemed to be an impossible task. Sharp pains jarred at her lower stomach, and despite the drugs, somewhere in some level of REM she could tell something was wrong.

Ara knew she had to wake up, her eyes still heavy from last night's tears. But if she forced them open, she would have to admit the ugly truth that this was now her reality. A widow at thirty, a misfortune she was going to eventually have to face head on. She pulled the plush blanket tighter around her body and drew in a deep breath before opening her eyes. Raina's claustrophobic excuse for an apartment seemed colder and more uninviting than usual. Wisps of hair that hung loose from her ponytail tickled her neck and face as the ceiling fan whirled and reminded her of Brad. He liked the fan on, she liked it off. The fan blew her hair just enough to keep her awake at night, an annoyance he could never quite understand. It seemed reasonable to her, he would never be able to sleep if she was tickling his neck relentlessly, but he'd seemed unable to understand her issue with it.

Ara pressed the irritating strands to her head and turned over. Something jumped out at her from the lowest shelf of the adjacent bookcase. A photo from Ara's very own wedding day, her entire bridal party looking *Knot Magazine* chic, laughing and smiling, facing off in different directions. One of those perfect un-posed wedding photos you hoped your group of drunk friends could pull off. She had loved the way she looked in her wedding dress. Next to her stood Lane, one hand on her shoulder, and to her right was Brad. Ara was staring ahead with an open mouth smile, her bouquet down at her side, the men on either side of her looking off in opposite directions.

Ara slid off the couch and crawled to the shelf on her knees and held the frame in her hands, tracing each face with her finger. She stared at the picture, laser-focused on her own beaming smile and perfectly swept back hair, secured loosely with a sparkling band. She had never felt as beautiful as she did on her wedding day, for once her entire look coming together exactly how she had envisioned. Maybe that was how she'd missed what she could see so clearly now, the uneasiness in

Brad's face, his eyes glancing off in the opposite direction, jaw clenched tight in an obligatory smile. How could she be so foolish to think he was happy? How did she convince herself that this man wanted a forever with her?

A high-profile marriage featured in the *New York Times*, flashy ring and a large apartment with a doorman was all she needed to shine with confidence. Brad and his family provided all of that. Had she looked past the obvious signs of trouble? Slumping back on the couch, she wondered why true happiness was too much to ask for, and closed her eyes again, falling back into a restless sleep. A life without Brad was a reality she was not willing to accept just yet.

Sometime later, Ara awoke to Raina tiptoeing around the apartment. Repeats of *Sex and The City* hummed in the background as she spoke quietly on the phone to someone, presumably their mother. Arabelle Ridener was probably still in California, debating whether or not to fly out. If her son-in-law's untimely death wasn't reason enough to fly to the east coast, Ara wondered what tragedy would have to unfold for her mother to justify it. *She'd probably even find an excuse for my own funeral.*

Her mother never came to New York. Ever. Her planned trips were always replaced with excuses and no shows. An advertising junky of the late eighties, her mother had had enough of New York and skipped off with the first ad man who turned Hollywood screenwriter she could latch onto. *How Pete Campbell of her,* Ara would often think nowadays. Obnoxiously, his name was even Peter.

Ara often blamed being a product of divorce—and being raised by her father and stepmom—for most of her adult insecurities. However, the truth was she hadn't minded her mother's absence. Arabelle was full of judgment, and the older Ara got, the less she cared to endure it. Her childhood wasn't perfect, but it was bearable, at least until her father passed away at the start of her senior year of high school. She was late as usual that morning and rushed through her routine and out to school without even saying a proper goodbye. She never imagined it would be the last time she saw him, sitting at their kitchen table, reading through his work email inbox while sipping his second cup of coffee. According to her stepmother, his heart attack lacked the dramatics of those in Hollywood; he simply fell to the floor, never to open his eyes again.

At the time, she would have barely considered her and her father close, but losing him more than proved that he meant the world to her. It was then, at just seventeen years old, that she learned the hard truth, that sometimes goodbyes could be forever.

She could assume raising a teenage girl wasn't easy, not that she tried to make it any easier on him. Ara was aware that she flirted with the line between normal and not. Her parents saw signs of it early, but given their preferred parenting technique—ignore and it will go away—they did nothing to help her until the day she learned she could act out. It was after one of her outbursts, after she threw one of her stepmother's prized antique vases onto the tile, that her father called Arabelle in California and begged for her to find someone on the east coast for Ara to talk to.

The ride into Manhattan, to Dr. Dan's that first time, was long and confrontational. Ara remembered screaming at her father that she didn't need a shrink, she needed a normal life. But he insisted she would come to love the sessions.

"It's an hour a week you get to talk about just you, sweetheart, who wouldn't enjoy that?"

Didn't he understand she never wanted to talk about herself?

Maybe he did, but knowing didn't stop her father. He marched her right into the building and up to the doctor's floor. After a heated argument in the hallway, a young Bradley Cooper lookalike came out from the office and introduced himself to her as Dr. Dan.

Ashamed of acting out in such a way in front of a near stranger, Ara regained her composure and walked into his office.

"Ara?" Dr. Dan's serene voice was calm and measured. Like he knew better than to place too much emotion behind his words, yet placed enough importance on them for her to trust him. She had just met him, but she already welcomed his soothing tone.

Realizing she was out of breath and sweating, Ara took a few deep draws of oxygen before answering, "I'm so sorry about that."

"For what?" said Dr. Dan. "I call that a Monday." Ara mustered out a quiet laugh through her labored breaths before retreating to the couch.

"You watch *The O.C.*? I hear Marissa and Ryan are on the outs again, huh?" Dr. Dan said.

Ara couldn't help laughing at his reference to *The O.C.* It was what she would later love about Dr. Dan, he always had a casual way about him that helped her realize things were not so bad. He managed to undermine demons with friendliness and indifference. Like nothing was new to him. Nothing was out of the norm.

"It's Trey's fault, Ryan's brother. He's a dick," Ara replied. Out of the corner of her eye, she saw Dr. Dan hushing her father from commenting on her inappropriate language.

"Every primetime show has one. Conflict keeps it interesting, don't you think?" said Dr. Dan before asking, "Wanna stay and chat for a little?"

"Sure, not my dad, though," she said. *I can't talk with him here.*

"But Ara—" said her father, who clearly was not understanding her need for personal space. Both her parents had a habit of twisting her issues into a personal attack on their parenting.

It wasn't too far after that when her father died. Dramatic or not, it was an event neither she nor her stepmother were prepared for and there wasn't a single moment where they pretended they would continue on without him. Her stepmom moved back with family in Iowa, and Arabelle returned to New York with her husband and Raina so Ara could finish out high school on the East Coast. There was some conversation about Ara moving out to California instead, mostly because, like Ara, Raina wanted to graduate with friends. For once, Arabelle put her daughter first, something Ara knew Raina always resented.

She could only imagine what her mother would have to say to her now, alone and widowed at such young age.

"I begged her to leave New York. What are people going to think about this," Ara could imagine her horrified mother saying as she hyped herself up over multiple glasses of wine club zinfandel.

Ara let her hand drop from the security of the blanket and searched for her cell phone on the floor, shifting the phone with her pointer finger until it was in reach. Typing in her pass code—her wedding anniversary—Ara prepared herself for what she was sure was going to be a flood of messages from over the past twenty-four hours. But there was nothing. Not one text or call. Not a single person had reached out to her. Not to console her, question her, or even just to confirm that she was alive herself. Not one.

Knowing that couldn't be, Ara threw off the blanket and stormed Raina's kitchen. She could see the horror on Raina's face as she nervously said she had to get off the telephone. Their mother still speaking as Raina hung up the call.

"What did you do!" Ara's face burned with anger. She could feel sweat gathering by the roots of her hair. "You deleted all of my messages and missed calls, I know you did! You have no right to go into my phone!"

Ara didn't wait for an explanation. She grabbed Raina's wrists and pulled her close but Raina lunged away and retreated to the caddy corner of the makeshift kitchen.

"You need to calm down, Ara, you're dealing with a lot right now. Please calm down!" Ara knew she should probably consider Raina's desperate plea but anger fueled her forward.

"That is my phone. MINE. It was not yours to poke your nose through and delete things as you wish. You have no right!" Ara screamed at Raina as she jumped from the counter top and tried her best to force Ara to retreat to the chair.

"You need to sit down, Ara. You have been through so many unimaginable things since last night. I'm only trying to help you, plus Mom thought it would be best for you not to read all that shit. I'm sorry, people just have so many opinions, you know that. People make things up," she said.

"Sure, and people also like to reach out and pay their respects and now I have no way of knowing who did that," Ara said through clenched teeth.

"We thought we were doing the right thing." Ara despised when Raina referred to her and Arabelle as *we*. It wasn't Ara's fault Raina never met her mother, and she could never understand why Raina wanted to latch herself onto hers.

"Do people really think I could do this?" Ara asked through her tears. "I loved him. He was everything to me. What messed up shit could people be saying that you felt you had to delete it all?"

"Of course not, Ara, I know you couldn't do it but think about how this looks to his family. They were never that fond of you in the first place, and they know the cops are going to start looking at you first. We know that they have to check you off before they can find the real douchebag who did this. But Brad's family is reading more into that than they should. Maybe it's easier than admitting it was random or a robbery or something."

40

"So you think you're saving me from Brad's family," Ara said, her retreating anger bubbling back to the surface. "I could handle the congressman, you had no right to make that decision for me."

"If we thought you should feed into it I wouldn't have deleted it. Please understand, it's easier not to react if you don't know at all, it was the right thing."

Again, with the WE.

"That's my decision, Raina! Get Mom back on the phone. I'm sure this was her idea," Ara yelled only to be cut off by Raina's shriek.

"Ara, oh my God. You're bleeding!"

Looking down, Ara saw the blood pooling at her center and in her pajama pants.

Stunned, she looked up at Raina, who had both hands cupped over her mouth in visible shock.

"Oh my God, Ara, you were pregnant."

Ara didn't even have to respond. It seemed Raina already knew the answer.

CHAPTER 6

When Lane first called her with news of the shooting, Raina was sure she would find Brad at the station, never thinking that he was the victim. Raina didn't think it was possible that Ara could be responsible, but what did she know? People snap, things go wrong. Sometimes people are simply not who you think they are. That's just human nature, right? Not every convicted murderer is a stone-cold serial killer. Hell hath no fury like a scorned lover, she remembered reading somewhere.

She knew Ara and what she could be capable of. She also knew Ara did not know Brad's secrets. Was there ever a way to truly know everything about a person's life? The Brad Bugia Raina knew was not a one-woman kind of man, let alone the marrying type. How manipulative he could be. He was from a family of politicians. Ara had to know at least portions of the truth about her husband.

Raina herself was no different, and she didn't even pretend to know anything about marriage. She was a withering addict to the attention and the challenge of luring someone in, controlling their every move, then discarding them like a used hand towel. People like her and

Brad thrived on the attention. Sure, he loved Ara. But Brad couldn't deprive his nature of who he was. Maybe that was what he saw in Ara. A person he was never going to be, a truly good person. A person who knew how to give everything to someone and to sacrifice. The Ying to his Yang. The calm to his storm.

But Raina saw who he really was and understood him perfectly. Two dark, self-centered souls feeding off the attention of others. Ara could never compete with that.

Maybe she did kill him, Raina thought. Nobody's perfect. Not even Ara, no matter how hard she tried. Wouldn't that be the kicker? A dark, deep-seeded fairytale of betrayal. The virtuous princess pushed to the edge of all edges. Pushed to murder.

She knew Ara would be furious that she deleted her messages, but Arabelle encouraged it, and that was good enough for her. Through the mix of somber texts, messages from friends, and forceful ones from Brad's family, one message stood out to her. Five simple words. *I've been trying to reach you.* It was all the text said, yet somehow it didn't seem to fit. The number was saved under a common name, Danielle, however Raina never heard Ara mention a friend or colleague with that name. Not once to her directly, but the texts had been coming since college—at least that's when Raina started noticing them. Wouldn't a best friend come to visit or make the pin board of pre-college photographs found in every freshman dorm room? Never wanting to directly ask Ara who Danielle was, she was left to wonder. If she asked about it, Ara would know that she was snooping, and that would take the fun out of it. She loved to virtually eavesdrop on Ara and report back to their mother. Phones do keep quite a bit of secrets.

While the other messages offered condolences or the typical ill-fated attempt at justifying the tragedy, the *he's in a better place* type, all Danielle's message said was *I've been trying to reach you*. No *I'm so sorry*. No *how are you*. But an urgent, *I've been trying to reach you*. The odder thing was, when Raina scrolled through the recent calls and text messages, Danielle had *not* been trying to reach Ara. Quite the opposite, Ara had called her, just once, the night Brad was killed. Hitting delete, Raina decided whatever Ara's secret was, she was going to cover it up for now.

CHAPTER 7

She lost their baby. Ara's final connection to Brad. A few weeks ago, she was elated with the news. They were finally going to have the family they always talked about.

"You are going to be an amazing mother one day when we're ready," Brad had said with a smile that always brought her to her knees. Compliments were particularly sweet coming from his lips, especially toward the end where they were few and far between.

Ara was cursed with a mother who resented that she managed to escape the womb unscathed from the lack of prenatal care. A daily scotch was hardly what the doctor recommended. That was exactly why Ara always wanted to be a loving maternal influence to a child. It would be the final proof that she was OK, that she had made it into adulthood despite her mother, who even in naming her, left the reminder that Ara would always be half as good in her eyes.

"But I'm going to get so fat," she had whined. "Burrito belly on steroids; who wants that?"

They'd both laughed at the thought. "When it happens, you'll be beautiful." Brad knelt on the kitchen floor and kissed her above her navel where a bump would have been. "Who doesn't love burritos?"

It was just weeks after confirming with her doctor that she was pregnant that the evil fist of the truth punched her in the gut. She could have lived forever not knowing what she knew now, that her husband was seeing someone else. The truth may set you free, but it was a hell of a lot easier to be kept in the dark. Maybe it was for the best not knowing. Being replaced is a hard pill to swallow.

The media chomped on the story like a piece of red meat at a July 4th barbecue, chewing and chewing until the flavor was sucked out, leaving nothing but tasteless commentary and overreaching opinions. If he were a different man, from a different family, the media may have passed on the story, but Brad being the only son of a New York congressman, especially during an election cycle, presented an opportunity for irresistible click bait. Theories flooded the news channels, each station offering up its own breaking details and exclusives. The viewer's tweets flashed across the bottom of the screen while the hard-nosed news anchors shredded Ara and Brad's relationship into slivers of falsities and pointed fingers in every direction.

The frenzy was expected of course, given the details. Young, successful couple in the prime of life, struck down by a horrific tragedy. America couldn't help but love a good mystery, especially when the horror fell upon those otherwise living charmed lives. It was as if watching the one percent suffer justified some personal disservice by God and balanced the scale.

At first Ara watched intently, starved like any other viewer for updates from the police. But as the coverage continued and the producers ran out of content to deliver, the stories pulled in character witnesses out of any rabbit hole from the couple's life. One by one, Ara watched as Brad's coworkers dished details of his office manner.

"Brad was the type that always said good morning," bragged one secretary. "Always complimenting something, your earrings, haircut, that sort of thing. A true gentleman."

Who the hell are you, and how do you know he was a gentleman? Ara would think as she obsessively Facebooked the Brittany's and Jessica's that claimed to be close friends and colleagues of her husbands, wondering who, if not all of them, were sleeping with him. Friends, of course, that he never mentioned over the typical how was your day dinner conversations they had. One woman went as far to say that although she assumed he had a happy marriage, she never heard him mention his wife nor did she ever see her in the office. Clearly alluding to trouble in paradise, just as the producers wanted. Obviously desperate to be asked back, or better, become a tabloid mistress and claim her five seconds of fame.

Ara noticed that, more and more, the special guests seemed heavily weighted in Brad's favor. As if the news outlets forgot that she was a core player in this sick and twisted storyline. While she denied the requests for comments originally, she never expected for the media to give up on her altogether. Was it easier to call in the acquaintances than his widowed wife?

It was only after his parent's televised press conference that the rumors started of shady deals he arranged for clients, or missing fundraising dollars collected as a political bundler. Finally, there was a new angle, whether true or not. If he didn't kill himself, and Ara was innocent, there had to be someone else, lying in wait for Brad Bugia to

48

key into his apartment, only to be destroyed by his own weapon. Someone who knew where to find the gun.

She was overjoyed when Raina said she had been contacted to be interviewed—at least it was someone for her corner. A public chameleon, Raina adapted to any role she was challenged with and had mastered the art of manipulation years ago. Confident Raina wouldn't betray her, Ara knew that if there was one thing Raina was good at, it was being the center of attention.

"I promise, Ar, I will show everyone how incredibly wonderful you are," she had said before going on air. "Everyone will love you and feel for you when I'm done."

Ara could not help thinking that it was an odd thing to say given the circumstances, but she chose not to overanalyze it. Did Raina think she needed people to feel for her? Did she know something Ara didn't?

Victimized by many the past few days, she wrote it off as being overly anxious, something she was prescribed Xanax for in her early twenties. But when the interview began to unfold on national television and she saw next to Raina in huge block lettering, Mutual Friend of

Victim and Wife, she no longer could talk herself out of the betrayal she felt.

Mutual friend? Raina and Brad saw a lot of each other and they were as close as any stepsister and husband, but Ara did not agree that mutual friend accurately reflected the threesome's relationship. She and Raina were stepsisters. Family. The girls' relationship was firmly cemented years before hosting any New Year's soirees. *How could she!* There was a never-ending line of special guests that were publically declaring their allegiance to Brad, his reputation did not need Raina. Ara needed Raina. The sting of her betrayal was sadly something Ara was accustomed to by now, but on national television?

Her ears hissed with anger as she listened to Raina's detailed version of her and Brad's love life. Flirtatiously skipping over detrimental questions that could have helped Ara.

"There had to be other women," the anchor questioned as Raina's glance shifted into a head tilting, corner glanced smirk.

"Brad was a very charming man, but he loved Ara. She was perfect for him," Raina responded.

"So there *was* cheating going on in the marriage? As a coworker, did you see anything you were uncomfortable with in the office? Anything you wanted to run home and tell your stepsister?" The network was going to run with this one, and Ara knew it. Raina, however, either lacked two brain cells to rub together or the attention was blinding her of any loyalty she had previously expressed.

"No, ma'am, if I did see anything, I knew it was harmless. Ara wouldn't have cared to know. She loves Brad and always trusted him."

Ma'am! And, of course, I would have cared to know. She was fuming.

She slammed the remote against the wall and pounded clenched fists against the couch. An uncomfortable gaze looked back at her from a canvas portrait of Raina she had displayed in her living room. A selfie of her on a beach that Ara always hated. There was something just plain gaudy about having your own face hanging on your walls. If anyone would do it, though, it would be Raina. *She probably gets off to herself,* Ara thought as the weathered couch suddenly seemed less inviting underneath her.

Picking up a lighter from the coffee table, she closed in on the image, disgusted by it more than usual. Slowly she held the lighter to Raina's face and watched as the pieces of fabric melted away, revealing a dark black hole. Ara sat back on the couch satisfied and lit the lavender candle on the coffee table. She'd have to throw that out before Raina got home.

CHAPTER 8

Brad's breath at the base of Raina's neck sent a shiver of excitement from her shoulders, down her arms, and piercing through her fingertips. The bathroom wall was cool as he backed her up against it, kissing first her neck, then chest, intensifying the sensations racing through her body. Cupping her breasts, his mouth moved up her body, kissing each spot until he was back at her lips.

In a single movement, he slipped her black lace panties to her ankles and pressed himself against her as she wrapped a leg around his waist. Forcing her leg back to the ground, he spun her in a complete one-eighty, her cheek now feeling the coolness of the wall. The air in the small bathroom pulsed with the intensity of getting caught as her body quivered and surrendered to her true cravings. Each thrust electrifying her need to be wanted. Knowing what he liked, she arched her back, pressing her bare bottom into him. Groaning, he finished and collapsed on top of her, inflated with the rush that comes with having someone you weren't supposed to. As their breathing slowed, she waited for the guilt she knew she should be feeling, yet never felt once after one of their secret rendezvous.

Raina knew not to sleep with a married man but doubted she was the first New Yorker to meddle with someone else's marriage. The guilt never came. If anything, she felt Ara deserved it, always playing by the rules. However, Brad seemed to regret their passionate trysts each time, which irritated her.

"She cannot find out. Ever. Understand me?" Brad said. "This would destroy her. I don't know who she would kill first, you or me."

Thinking of Ara killing *her* made Raina laugh out loud. "You think she could take me? Nah, you would just have to deal with her all sad and crying," she said, pouting at him with a fake frown.

She knew damn well Brad was not hers, and she never expected him to be. More importantly, she wasn't entirely sure she wanted him to be. That would spoil their undeniable attraction. It was the danger of being with Brad that ignited something deep in the pit of her insecurities. Yes, he was good-looking, successful, and could screw like an A-lister in a Hollywood movie, but it was the feeling of power and being second to no one, not even his wife, that she loved. The fact the he

54

would risk it all—his entire life with Ara, for a five-minute romp in a New York bar—who wouldn't be turned on by that?

"She never has to know," Raina said as she secured her panties back in place. Taking one reassuring glance in the mirror, she wiped a smear of lipstick from the corner of her lips. In a blur of confidence, she returned to the cocktail party and her best friend.

"You dirty little thing, you!" Ara said as Raina approached her. "You are practically screaming that you just screwed. You and James again?" *If you only knew.*

James and Brad walked toward the girls with fresh glasses of prosecco, Brad giving a slight wink to Ara that she returned with a content smile.

"You'd be surprised," Raina said as she playfully poked James above his belt buckle.

"I do not even want to know. You're one of kind!" Ara said as the foursome clicked glasses and continued into the ease of a night out with friends.

You're right, Raina thought. *You do not want to know.*

CHAPTER 9

Detective Benjamin Maro stared at the file that lay open amongst the clutter of take-out containers and unclosed cases making up the mess he called his desk. As a detective in a major metropolitan area like Jersey City, he was not new to the mystery and frustration of a case going cold, but he could not seem to let the Brad Bugia case go. No matter how many times he slammed the file shut, concluding the poor son-of-a-bitch had did it himself, the file and its details would taunt him until he reopened it. Sure, it was the victim's gun, but it didn't mean he had to be the one who pulled the trigger. If his day was slow, he would peek back into the file, intrigued by each detail of the haunting death of such a promising young man.

Maybe it was Bugia's pretty little wife; Ara Hopkins could probably sway Elton John back to the straight man's side. Image after image of the young widow lay in front of him, looking like she stepped out of some wholesome primetime television sitcom from back in the day, not the nonsense they fill the timeslot with now, chock full of vampires and teen drama. But did her beauty mean she was innocent? *No one is that good on the inside and outside.*

Although a genuinely passionate cop, Maro was known to push the boundaries. He was also known to be compulsive and passionate when convinced of someone's guilt. While his gut instincts were often spot on when it came to the street thugs and dealers that crowded his city, the high profile, high society cases seemed to get to his head. As if there was a score that needed to be settled between the upper crust and himself.

Maro shuffled his mouse causing the screen to kick back up from sleep mode, revealing Ara's bare-boned Facebook page. Her page lacked the details that others from her generation posted on the social site, yet he scrolled down through the now-familiar photos and posts, hoping he would find something revealing if he just looked a little bit deeper. He didn't know a soul this day and age with a squeaky clean digital presence; there was always some sort of dirt somewhere. He was sure of it. He just hadn't found it yet.

Maro took a bite of his Mama's Chicken Fra Diavlo—not homemade, of course; Mama's was the dingy corner spot near the station—he stopped mid-chew and stared at one of the comments posted after Brad's death. A Dr. Daniel DaVedere said, *"My heart goes out to you, Ara. And to think all you have overcome."* The comment, vague yet too significant to ignore, was closed with a simple, *"I'm here."* No contact info, no other details.

Maro sat straight up and stared closer at the screen. *Now who the hell are you, Dr. Daniel DaVedere from New York, New York? And what has Ara overcome?*

Clicking into a second tab, Detective Maro pulled up his Google browser and carefully copied the doctor's name into the bar, clicking to reveal all the internet had to offer. Dr. Daniel DaVedere was a psychologist serving the five boroughs, with an "innovative, hands-on approach in tackling minor to severe mental illnesses."

Maro scrolled through the various pages of the psychologist's templated website, surprised to learn that Dr. DaVedere did not treat couples. "Due to Dr. Dan's ground-breaking and unique tactics, we prefer to counsel all ages strictly one on one." Ara must have seen him alone.

And to think all you have overcome apparently did not mean as a couple. Maro disliked the guy already. With just one look at his headshot he could tell he was a douchebag. Just the fact that he referred to himself as "Dr. Dan" irked him. Like he was trying to appeal to you in a neighborly, guy-next-door fashion. In his early forties, his face showed minimal signs of aging, his lines likely concealed by expensive fillers. *What a jerk-off,* Maro thought. The doctor had the type of face you couldn't help but want to punch.

Taking screenshots of the Facebook comment and anything on the doctor's website or personal Facebook page that flat out rubbed him the wrong way, Maro printed them out on the old, beat up '90s communal office printer and tucked the sheets of paper into the file, then turned back to the photos of Ara. *What are your secrets, Ara Hopkins? What did you overcome?*

His cell buzzed on the desk next to him.

"Maro," he said, still staring at the photographs. "What do you mean you got something?"

He grabbed his keys and shoveled a final bite of Mama's into his mouth. "Just wait right there. Don't do anything. I'm on my way." And with that, Maro was out the door and off to the forensics lab processing evidence from the Bugia case.

If his gut feeling was right and this was more than a suicide, this could be just the case he needed to polish the smudge from his reputation.

Maro forced his way through the double doors at the downtown forensics lab without an ounce of grace in his step. His younger partner, Detective Jason Ameno, was involved in an intense conversation with the forensics expert assigned to the case. They all turned to Maro when he walked in, seemingly anxious to share what they had.

Ameno jumped in as the tired, veteran forensics examiner dutifully took the back seat. "The gun was registered to Brad Bugia. The victim, we know that," Ameno said.

As if he didn't know that already. Tipping his neck from side to side, Maro took a deep breath, calming his more irritable side. He was not a fan of working as a team, especially when his partner seemed to align their working relationship with that of college fraternity brothers. Poking and prodding about what Maro did the night before while he bragged about the blackout blowjobs he got from wasted twentysomethings he met at the Hoboken bars. He'd prefer to save reminiscing on personal matters for when he was alone at home and just stick to doing his job when he was at work. Events in his rearview mirror were easier to accept when no one was there to judge him.

"Were there any prints besides his own?" There was nothing wrong with knocking him down a notch or two. The forensics examiner, hardened with years of experience, recognized the power move and smiled at her baby boomer ally.

Ameno cleared his throat and said, "That's the best part, there are three confirmed and one partial. His, hers, the best friend detective, and an unknown partial."

Maro's face tightened as he turned to the forensics examiner. "So we got Brad, Ara, Lane, and a partridge in a pear tree? That's great. The owners of the firearm, a NYPD detective, and an unknown? Not to mention, it matches up with what Ms. Hopkins and Bene told us. What the heck am I going to do with that?"

"I'm not in the mood, Detective," said the examiner, a quirky five-foot-nothing fireball of a women from the Bronx. Maro suspected she was thinking something along the lines of *asshole detectives.* "But since I like my job, unlike you miserable folks, I will tell you that the two gentlemen's prints were found near the trigger, and the victim's prints were also found in a defensive position, such as this, as if you were trying to get the gun away from someone." She mimicked the motion.

"And Ara Hopkin's?"

"Not on the trigger, but you do have her holding the weapon."

"I knew it wasn't suicide, we're gonna get her on this." Maro grabbed the file from the examiner and literally patted Ameno on the back. This was his favorite part of the job, when his gut instincts rang true.

"I wouldn't be so sure, Detective. The only full prints near the trigger are from the vic and Detective Lane Bene," she said, now moving him down a peg or two. "And then there is the partial that's not in the system."

Ameno jumped in, "And I found a figure on the security footage. I followed up, knocked on some doors, and haven't been able to cross it off. We may have someone in the building who wasn't supposed to be there."

The gratification from learning about the prints was replaced with a boiling sense of rage. *Why can't I catch a goddamn break?* Maro knew he wasn't wrong with this one. It wasn't the friend or Brad or an unknown. It was little Miss Ara Hopkins. He was positive, and it would take a lot to convince him otherwise. Although he reminded himself that he had felt this way before, and unfortunately it wouldn't be the first time he'd been wrong. This time was different, though. It had to be. Other times, he had been sloppy, drank a little too much, or was distracted by immature relationship drama, the type where your only choice at the end is to play the *it's not you, it's me* card. But he hadn't had a sip of hooch in over a year, and he sure was steering clear from any type of nonsense distractions he couldn't afford to have in his life. Not if he wanted to keep his job. The chief had made sure that was clear. And thanks to free internet porn and an occasional hook up who was impressed with his badge, he didn't need anything of real significance. He could get by as he was just fine.

"One more thing before you go. I got the subpoena for the emails from the firm," Ameno said as he handed Maro a thick envelope overflowing with what he hoped was straight juice.

Scanning through the top few pages, *we got her,* was all Maro could think.

Unfortunately, Martina Hernandez, the District Attorney residing over their corner of Jersey, didn't see it the same way. "What do you have on her? I don't have to remind you that you need hard evidence to make an arrest, Detective, do I?" She walked over to the detectives, grabbing the emails from Maro's hands.

The detective paced back and forth, rubbing his forehead. "Her prints are on the gun, I told you. There's more there, Hernandez, we just need time."

"So what?" she countered. "It was her husband's gun. Didn't Bene say he taught them both how to use the weapon, that explains three of the four prints. You are not giving me anything to work with here."

Martina Hernandez was known for being tough on crime and even tougher on the men who were on her side. "I just need more time, Hernandez, please," Maro begged. He knew she wouldn't allow such a controversial case to be tried on circumstantial evidence alone, but he'd had to try. No jury would convict Ara Hopkins on a single fingerprint that any decent defense attorney could explain away.

"Time is not something I can give you, Ben." Maro hated when she called him by his first name. She only did so when her virtuous, motherly side was coming out—or when she wanted him to remember that his cases were nothing without her approval. She was calling him Ben much more often now, after the incident. It almost cost her *her* career the last time, and like any obedient dog, she had learned from her mistakes.

Maro knew Hernandez could see the fixation in his face, and he knew it wasn't good. He had to be levelheaded. Act like he was no more invested than he needed to be.

"This is what happened before. You dig and dig and dig until you lose sight of reality," she said more firmly. "You need to let this one go for now. You get more evidence, other than a partial print or whatever the hell you got, fine. But for now, this conversation is over." Martina Hernandez turned on her heel. "I mean it, Maro. It can't be like last time. You have nothing on Ara Hopkins, nothing that'll stick." At least he was back to his last name. She must not be too mad at him.

She was right. It couldn't be like last time. His gut had been contaminated last time, poisoned by Johnny Walker. He hadn't been able to think straight, in a constant fog from being drunk or hungover. But it wasn't about being obsessed with that case, it was about proving his own worth. He'd *needed* to solve that case—for himself, not just for the victims and their family. Corners had been cut, and a few formalities overlooked. And yes, an innocent girl had almost ended up in jail. But at the time, those were small infractions compared to closing the case.

Yet his mistakes had cost him everything he'd ever cared about. Somehow, he had managed to mend the situation professionally, but at immeasurable loss to his personal life. His divorce had stripped him of everything: his wife, twin boys, and half his pension. Hell, she got the house and all that was in it, too. If only he'd been in a better state to fight at that time, for his marriage and for himself. Things could've been so different.

But that was then, and almost three years had passed. He'd taken advantage of the court-ordered rehabilitation and stood with the other drunks every Tuesday in the basement of St. Catherine's, repeating the mantra, "Hi, my name is Ben Maro, and I'm an alcoholic," as if it was something he would ever forget or forgive himself for. It took a while, but finally he'd regained unsupervised visitation with his twins. Or he would, if they'd ever agree to see him, which so far they refused to do. *One day.* Today, he had to find more evidence in this case.

"Tell me more about this mysterious figure, Ameno."

"Dammit, Hernandez, are we really gonna get jammed up on a dark spot on the security footage, give me a break."

"Well, Ben, I'm no detective, but an unknown person, unknown prints, and a stack of emails filled with financial details, political players, and, if I'm reading correctly, some very *saucy* office affairs. Looks to me like you got some more work to do."

CHAPTER 10

It was a week after the funeral, and thanks to the cocktail of anxiety and depression medication Ara washed down with black coffee each morning, she was slowly adjusting to her new life. Still not able to return to her apartment or her advertising job at NBC, Ara's days were filled with reruns and rearranging her few things in the cramped corner of Raina's apartment she occupied. Her once-healthy 128-pound figure was disappearing, leaving more and more room in her sagging clothes. Her hair, now always secured in a tight bun, desperately needed to be tended to, and her manicure was chipped away.

Every day, Raina brought home moderately-priced takeout meals and cued up the cheesy horror movies they used to enjoy together in a desperate attempt to entertain her. But a part of her died with Brad that cold winter day in their now empty apartment, and with their baby. And nothing Raina could do would change that. Ara was mourning more than her young husband. She was mourning the loss of pieces of herself.

Her mother flew in from the West Coast and spent an astonishing entire week at The W in a mild effort to console her. With only a few disapproving comments, Ara almost enjoyed the pity-filled time they spent together. A very tactical and analytical woman, Arabelle guided Ara through the many post-tragedy annoyances that needed to be dealt with, such as working with Brad's parents in planning the funeral. An event Ara would have loved to keep on the small side, but was overruled by both mothers.

The entire thing had felt suffocating. From standing over Brad's grave, cringing at each pair of eyes lashing out at her with their opinions on whether she could have killed the well-loved Brad Bugia to Ameno and Maro's presence that only increased the judgment. Nothing, especially two men lacking custom tailored suits, got by the movers and shakers Brad's family engaged with. All she could do was hope her natural anxiety wasn't poking holes in the grieving widow appearance her mother put together.

She was also horribly imprisoned in her own mind. The thought of Brad's body spending eternity tucked six feet under the ground caused her own body to ache with anguish. The depressing finality of the culture's version of resting in peace. Wasn't it more romantic to scatter one's ashes at sea? Toss ourselves from our favorite bridge in one last true effort at freedom and wanderlust. The morbid act of locking our loved ones in an overpriced box, tossing a few handfuls of dirt and leaving them at the will of a gravedigger to pat down the dirt and finish the deed curdled her stomach.

After, the group returned to the Bugia's home for Chardonnay and a cheese plate, comforted in the thought that Brad would want them to smile and feel happiness. When in reality, everyone was silently relieved they weren't the ones buried under ground.

Ara didn't think for one second that Brad would've wanted her to smile. If there was an afterlife, there was no way Brad was up there wishing her well. He had grown tired of her here. There was no way in heaven or hell that after being released from his human responsibilities he was thinking of her at all. Wine in hand, she wondered if everyone who clutched her shoulders and offered their condolences had seen through the flaws in their marriage from the beginning. Brad was looking for a way out. And ironically, in death, he got one.

The Bugia's walked through the motions of supportive in-laws, even though Ara knew, they would have avoided her all together if they weren't obsessively maintaining their reputation. They never said it publically, but made it clear through their actions they thought she had something to do with Brad's death. At one point, from across the room, she swore she saw the congressman ask Lane if he thought she did it. Lane's eyes caught hers, and he offered a kind smile before excusing himself and crossing the room to meet her.

Embracing her in a friendly hug he whispered, "You're doing fine," before continuing to greet the mutual friends scattered about the room. An off remark, but she guessed he saw through her façade and into her true discomfort in the situation. The attention on her alone was too much to bear. Let alone the vicious stares from those who were convinced of her involvement.

Her mother, on the other hand, wanted Ara to get back to a 'new normal,' as she called it and made it quite clear she did not believe in wallowing. The dirt had barely settled over Brad's grave, and there was her mother telling her it was time to saddle up and stop moping, she needed to find a man to take care of her. "I could have wallowed when things went south with your father," she'd said, "but I powdered my nose, fixed my hair and found myself Peter. Now look at my life and all that I have! Losing your father was practically the best thing that ever happened to me."

"You *left* Dad for Peter, Mom," Ara had spit through clenched teeth. "You left both of us. Not the same as coming home to find your husband shot dead in your living room."

Her mother had shrugged and busied herself folding clothes and picking up around her stepdaughter's apartment. Ara was surprised she didn't have her on Meet.com days after the memorial service. However, if left to her mother, it would probably be millionaire matchmaker. Ara was over wishing their relationship was different—that her mother would provide some sort of real comfort like others did. Other mothers were not Arabelle Ridener.

"All I am saying is that you have no idea what is even out there. I thought your father was it for me. Same for you and Brad. But oh my, Peter! The things he did to me that your father forgot all about. He'd have me against his desk. Here I would be thinking he was just in it to get off, and he'd drop to his knees and lift my skirt . . ."

"Mom!" Disgusted, Ara had heard enough.

"Darling, you need to grow up. It's just a little oral."

"Ugh! Who even uses that word!" Ara pushed the covers off of her and pulled sweatpants over her Target brand, full butt panties. Even if Raina could shrug it off, hearing these words coming out of her mother's mouth made her want to throw up, and she was content with that making her the prude of the family.

"Maybe if you let Brad explore you down there, wore some lingerie instead of whatever those things are," she said pointing toward Ara's granny panties, "things would have been different."

Ara swallowed the obvious words begging to torpedo from her mouth. No amount of head on either of their parts could have stopped Brad from being murdered in their own home. It did not matter if he'd wanted more from her in the bedroom, he apparently had no problem getting what he wanted away from home.

Thankfully, her mother helped in other ways. She filed the life insurance claim despite Ara's desperate pleas that doing so would only make her look guilty. But her mother demanded.

"He had this insurance for a reason, Ara. So that if, God forbid, something like this happened to him, you would be taken care of," she had said. "He wouldn't want you to suffer any more than you had to."

73

He was a good man in that respect, her mother would chirp as she excitedly spoke of her thirty-year-old daughter starting over. Arabelle viewed Brad as a financial transaction from the start, not once pretending they would live happily ever after and was quick to point out the obvious downfalls to dating one of New York's most eligible bachelors.

"There is no such thing as a faithful man who looks like that with pockets that deep," she would say "they don't have to be good to you or respect you. Women wait in line to screw 'em," she'd say, crossing some imaginary mother/daughter boundary Ara set up in her head.

Whether he was all good, part good, or no good, Ara did not want what she thought of as Brad's blood money. No matter how many times Raina or her mother reassured her that was not what it was, she could not get past that he had to die for her to receive the payout. Sure, the million-dollar policy was nice but she would pay double to get him back and have the life they were supposed to. She had so many questions she wanted to ask him, despite knowing he would have a typical Brad Bugia, well-practiced defense so reasonable she wouldn't be able to do anything but agree with. At least she could have heard it directly from him.

To no one's surprise, the police called within days of the policy being filed and began looking deeper into the couple's financial affairs. Too bad "I told you so" had zero effect on Arabelle. Even when wrong she would fight imprudently that she was right.

At least, to Ara's knowledge, there was nothing for the police to find. Brad may have had his secrets when it came to women, but she would know if they were financially in trouble, wouldn't she? It's not like she planned on spending a cent of it anyway.

When the congressman texted her that he was glad his son was at least prepared financially for his death, she could practically taste the sourness in his words. If the family and its posse were closed off to her before, it was bound to only get worse with Brad's death.

CHAPTER 11

Arabelle was on her way back to California, promising to return within a few weeks to 'check up on her.' Ara knew better than to expect a repeat visit, and settled into a life with Raina's couch and DVR. Tuesdays were Ara's favorite. Such an insignificant day to the rest of working America that the television networks were practically begging for viewers. Hoping some desperate housewife was home feeling as unfulfilled as she was, the stations would play syndicated 'classic' shows that hooked the thirtysomethings and dragged them right back into their own adolescent, carefree years. Oh, to have the problems of the wealthy teens on *The O.C.* and *One Tree Hill.*

The Orange County high school lovebirds, Ryan and Marissa, were foolishly quarreling over another miniscule early 2000s conflict when Ara heard a knock at the door. Raising the volume, she was now a master at ignoring any type of interaction with the outside world. The knock rang again and this time she recognized the voice on the other side. "Ara, open the door." It was Lane.

Pausing the DVR, she sluggishly walked to the doorway and was greeted with his warm smile.

"Hey there, princess. Can I come in?"

Already slightly irritated by his sarcasm, Ara said, "Sure. If you never, ever call me princess again."

"Deal." Lane brushed passed Ara, unfazed by her remark as she followed him back through the living space and returned to her spot on the couch. She pointed the remote and un-paused the television only for it quickly to be paused again by Lane.

"I am here to take you out. You need to get out of this apartment. Anything you want, we will do it," he said placing a hand on hers.

Ara pushed his hand away and leaned back on the couch. "Please don't do this, Lane. I just want to sit here and watch ridiculous television with ridiculous plots and not think about the fact that my husband is dead," she said, her voice shaking slightly when saying the word: *Dead.*

Lane looked back at her like he was expecting that answer and retreated toward the front door, grabbing two brown bags that he carried back into the apartment.

"I had a feeling you would say that, so here's Plan B." He placed the bags on the coffee table and removed a large bottle of one of Ara's favorite California reds, a bottle of scotch, and Chinese takeout. "Pick your poison," he said.

Drinking before noon was not a typical Tuesday afternoon for her, not even for this "new normal," but she was surprised to find herself considering her options. Times had changed, and she embraced the opportunity to numb her mind. Never a scotch drinker and a self-proclaimed wine-o since her early twenties, she was even more shocked when she reached toward the heavier, quick-hitting option. She needed something strong.

Lane poured two large glasses of scotch into the red solo cups he had in the brown bag and handed one to Ara. He playfully clicked her plastic cup before consuming a large sip. Ara mimicked his motion and took down a large gulp of the bitter drink, the scotch burning the back of her throat in a surprisingly satisfying way.

Lane opened a few of the Chinese takeout containers and handed her the lo mein, Ara's favorite dish.

"Let's eat it like in the movies. Right out of the container," Lane said as he threw a pair of chopsticks in Ara's direction.

Ara laughed a little as she fumbled with the utensils and said, "Why do they always do that, anyway? I mean, I've never actually seen someone do that in real life."

Lane took a second sip of scotch and chased it with a heaping portion of pork fried rice. "Well, apparently, we do." His eyes locking with Ara's, he smiled.

Again, Ara mimicked Lane's motions and laughed, feeling more comforted than she had felt in weeks. Lane was the closest thing she had to Brad, and it helped that she had always genuinely felt at ease with him.

"So what did I miss?" Lane asked as he adjusted himself on the couch.

He stayed there through much of the afternoon. Chuckling occasionally at the pure nonsense of the show and the unlikely conflicts the main characters found themselves in.

By three in the afternoon, Ara was heavily intoxicated and almost enjoying herself for the first time in weeks. Lane seemed uncharacteristically into the teen drama, hanging on the edge of his seat each time one of the show's regular couples broke up for the umpteenth time.

Ara allowed herself to lean on Lane and found solace in his toned, inviting arms. Maybe it was the scotch, or the overall dramatics of the teen soap playing out in front of her, but for the first time in weeks she let down her guard.

"They think I killed Brad, Lane," she said matter-of-factly. "I know they do."

"Who is they, Ara?"

"The police, his parents. I feel like everyone thinks I had something to do with it."

Lane hesitated carefully considering her statement. "Well, did you," he said, not quite as a question before adding, "of course you couldn't have. You loved him, Ara. Everyone knew that."

The two sat in silence, both contemplating the thought.

"You're wrong, Lane. People have been known to kill those they love. And to be honest, I think I could have if I needed to," Ara said, staring blankly ahead, her eyes dry. Lane grabbed the scotch from her hand.

"Stop saying stuff like that, Ar. You could not have. And you didn't need to, so what you need to do is stop saying things like that." Lane pulled at her shoulders until she was facing him. His eyes desperately searched for any emotion on her face.

"He was with someone else. I know he was, I don't know who, but I know there was someone else," Ara said, turning back to her Johnny Walker.

"Stop it, Ara. Where is this coming from? Maybe this nonsense isn't good for you," Lane said, waving at the TV, "watching this dramatic shit all day. You should be seeing someone, speak to a therapist." He put his hand back on her knee.

Leaning her head to his chest, she said, "I'm talking to you. Therapists, they don't do anything for you except make it worse and bring up old shit you don't want to talk about."

Lane smiled and gave her thinning frame a squeeze. Ara reached for the scotch bottle with her free hand and took a drawn-out sip, feeling a sense of peace.

She had been too afraid to confront Brad and find out who he was seeing because her dreams of starting a family with him were finally coming true. She had hiked those stairs in her beautiful new heels that she adored and had paid for herself. By the time she got to the top she knew the answer to the question she had been toying with in her mind for weeks. She had an idea who he was going to leave her for and all she needed from him was to confirm it. Say it to her face.

"Let's trade fortunes," Lane said, clearly changing the subject in an attempt to break the awkward silence. They each scooped a cookie in their hands and handed each to the other.

Ara's fortune looked back at her from the tiny sliver of paper: *Welcome the beautiful changes coming into your life.* Beautiful? She crumpled the fortune, tossing it in the garbage bag, and took another swig from the bottle.

"Not a good one?" Lane said.

"It's just a cookie," she replied, retreating back into silence.

CHAPTER 12

She stopped at the corner liquor store before going back to her and Brad's old apartment, expecting the bottle of wine she purchased to at least make her groggy. Sleeping seemed more of a luxury these days than a necessity. Back here, her world was too cold and uninviting for something as relaxing as sleep and rest. It wasn't the bed that she and Brad once shared, and it wasn't that she was afraid to turn off the lights or even that someone could take her own life as easily as they took Brad's. Ara was afraid to turn off her mind, fearing the vulnerability of sleep. Now more than ever, she needed to be in control, to be calculated and clear. Not muddled down with feelings. Every emotion she allowed the world to see needed to be in check and on par with the expected behaviors of a new widow, taking every proper step on the road to a life after a loved one's death. That was how to reclaim normality. Do this, and others can provide their sugary stamp of approval. She could be back to the "normal" everyone was so desperately yearning for her to return to.

Ara could still remember the exact moment she realized the power of her female sexuality and the control she could wield with it. After many sleepless nights filled with Googling anything and everything about sex and educating herself through whispers of pornography and late-night episodes of MTV's *Undressed*, she'd finally felt ready to seduce the man she adored. She was sure Dr. Dan felt exactly as she did but had more than a few reasons to restrain himself from giving in to his urges. His reputation, professional license, and freedom, to name a few. But Ara was confident she could break though *his* shell and inhibitions. She wanted to feel control.

And she could reclaim that control now hopefully, back in her apartment, heading back to her same old job, and back to what was a glimpse of her old life. To the world, she was recovering at an acceptable pace. *How sad*. Ara wasn't exactly sure what emotions of hers were real and which ones were simply part of her plan to get out from under the microscope that was her mother and Raina. Almost six weeks at her stepsister's apartment was far too long. Now back in her own place she could have some sort of control over her life, and she welcomed that. At times, she missed the control more than she missed

84

him. She needed control. She breathed in control like oxygen, keeping her alive until the next breath.

Now here she was, lying awake in the middle of the night, her mind blurred from overanalyzing her past and her morbid future of being alone. Memories of then swirled in her head, mixed with the pain of her present situation. How did she manage to lose her father, who she never gave a chance, and her husband, who she gave too many?

But oh, how she missed Brad. Despite her mother's attempts to erase him from the apartment with expensive cleaning crews and interior designers. She longed for the life he'd promised—the comfort of it. Someone to witness her own life. Someone who made her normal. All of it now taken from her in a single instant. In a blink of an eye her life had changed forever. There was no going back now.

Ara's phone shook against the rich oak nightstand. A text from Lane flashed onto the screen.

Let me guess . . . Sheep 1,176,524. After a few nights of casual texting, he knew she would be awake at 2am.

Lord knows what the actual count would be if she had actually been counting sheep, but she typed back, *spot on.*

Ara felt a little guilty that she and Lane were closer than ever since Brad's death. It was one of the things Arabelle and Raina would definitely have something to say about. Maybe that was why she welcomed it, or maybe it was that Lane reminded her of Brad. Or maybe the mutual pain from Brad's death lingered between them, connecting them like long lost lovers. Either way, Ara didn't care what people thought at this point. Lane brought her comfort.

Her phone buzzed again. *I'm in the area, I can stop in if you're lonely.*

Hoping that he was already on his way, she playfully waited to respond, less than patiently.

She wondered what her mother or Raina would say about her allowing him to come over, even if it was a plot line found in multiple Lifetime movies and romantic comedies: needing comfort post tragedy, leading lady finds herself falling into some other man's arms. Hollywood had made millions, probably billions, on the concept. So why couldn't she benefit from it as well?

The three loud bangs on her front door startled her. She had given Lane a key in anticipation of a situation like this.

She wrapped herself in her bathrobe and fixed her hair as she passed the hall mirror.

It wasn't Lane at the door.

"Raina? What's the matter?" Raina looked a mess. Her hair stuck to her forehead, framing her mascara-smeared face. Layers of caked on MAC products gathered in the corners.

"You're my best friend, Ara, you know that. You are the sister I never had, and I love you."

Ara wrapped her arms around her, Raina's wet face finding a place on her shoulder. *Only she could get this drunk on a weekday.* "What's this about? Of course, we're sisters. Forever, remember?"

"You are going to hate me one day, and I'm going to have no one." Her hysterics kicked up as she snorted through her nose to breathe, unsteady on her feet.

"Why would I hate you? Don't be ridiculous. I don't have a reason to, now do I?"

Unsure what to say other than that, Ara let her cry. She had learned years ago that when Raina was wasted, it was best not to provide any real advice or concern. Raina would rile herself up and then pass out, only to wake tomorrow angry that her eyes were puffy.

"Promise me you will never hate me."

"I can't think of a reason why I would."

Raina didn't look up as she walked her over to the sofa, covering herself with the softest blanket. Ara went to the kitchen, returning moments later with a glass of water, only to find Raina had slipped out, leaving behind nothing but mascara trails on Ara's throw pillow.

Typical. Ara took a sip of the water and went back to the bedroom. She sat on the end of the bed, brushing her hair over her shoulders. The front door slammed and Lane appeared in her bedroom doorway.

"What, did you miss me?" he said. Ara stood, her loose tank top slipping off her shoulder, nearly revealing her right breast. It didn't need to be said, the truth was she did miss Lane. But her words, those were still Brad's for now.

"Are you all right?"

She took a few steps toward him and reached her arms around his waist. He stood stock still at first, then wrapped his arms tightly around her as she let her fingertips trace lines up his back. She felt his body tense with anticipation of what could come. Lane leaned down and lightly kissed the nape of her neck.

"We can talk if you want," he said softly, but she didn't need to talk.

She needed the attention he was willing to give her. Each touch left her wanting to explore a little bit more of him. They turned and he sat on the bed, pulling her in. Not understanding everything she was feeling, she held the back of his head and kissed him. Hard and despairing. Maybe it was the wine, or the depressing thought of being alone, but Lane felt exactly like what she needed right now. She caught a glimpse of them in the floor-length mirror hanging on the opposite wall. Not wanting to feel any ping of guilt, she said through heavy breaths, "Can you get the light?" Once blanketed in darkness, Ara pulled him into her bed, and he followed willingly, lying down behind her, wrapping a single arm around shoulders. Ara with her back against him, closed her eyes.

"It will all work out," Lane whispered before kissing her one more time at the base of her neck in between her shoulders.

"I hope so, Lane," she said, before finally falling asleep.

CHAPTER 13

With a single step off the Path train, Ara was overcome by the stench steaming from the city streets. Oh, how she'd missed New York. The very essence of so much success and failure compacted into one small island invigorated her. At any moment you could turn down a new street and walk straight into a new life. Taking in one more smog-filled breath, she started toward her office, which sat comfortably near Rockerfeller Center on Sixth Ave.

"You are simply not ready to go back," her mother said in the calls they shared prior to today. But two months seemed plenty long for Ara. She knew if the situation were reversed, her mother would wallow in the pity of others as long as it lasted and then some. "Moving on sure, but back to work?" she said. "It may just be too much, sweetie." But thankfully, Ara could stand on her own two feet. Raina, of course, tried to fight her mother's battle on this side of the continent, but Ara knew how to handle both of them. Instead of allowing them the drama, she simply continued along her morning routine, pulled her long hair back into a sophisticated knot, and was on her way back to the life she once knew.

She whisked through the lobby, pausing only to scan her ID badge before continuing through the turnstile and onto the elevator. Before she knew it, she was on the thirty-seventh floor, where she had spent most of her time over the past few years. But when the doors opened, she wasn't greeted by a warm smile from Kara, the receptionist, whose presence had always been a comfort to her in yesteryears, but instead by the sight of Detectives Maro and Ameno casually leaning on a desk in the left corner of the entryway. Kara bustled about, trying not to notice the obviously unwelcome detectives, and awkwardly struggled to avoid eye contact with Ara.

"Ms. Hopkins," her boss, Ryan, said through the glass doors. "A word, please."

Once in his office, Ara suddenly felt uncomfortable with his anything but welcoming demeanor. She barely understood a word he said, the words moving in one ear and out the other, until she heard the ones she was dreading.

"We are so sorry, Ara, we really are," he said. "We just can't have this much attention on the network right now. With the merger and all. Not to mention the time you took off." His eyes held a heavy glaze of disapproval and maybe even a hint of flat out disgust. Ara wished he would just be straight with her, instead of his feeble attempt at compassionate conversation. Tell her she was a possible suspect in the city's hottest murder investigation and that they needed to create distance to avoid scandal at the network.

Prior to Brad's death, Ara had a wonderful working relationship with Ryan, and everyone else at her job, for that matter. They had moved up together for years, him a rung ahead on the corporate ladder. Countless times he talked her off a ledge when an ad buy she was handling ran during the wrong programming. Ryan was at the network longer then her, but not long enough to actually be out of her professional league, they always seemed to be in the mud together. No matter how bad it was, or how ridiculous a client or sales representative acted, Ryan helped Ara laugh off the stresses of the advertising world. Typically, with a cat meme or twerking viral video.

But now, in her lowest of lows, he seemed disgusted to be associated with her. And sitting in his office, Ara could not help but feel the sting of his disapproval. *Innocent until proven guilty, my ass.* The media should have just crucified her in Times Square during Christmas time. Everyone thought she was guilty anyway, why not put on a show.

Unaware of the protocol, Ara stood, "I guess I'll get my things then."

"Kara has a box out front for you. We had her pack up your desk yesterday to avoid a scene. I'm sorry, Ara, I really am."

The box was waiting at Kara's desk when she came back into the welcome area. All of her belongings from years of hard work, tucked away in a single printer paper delivery box. Maro looked more than satisfied that her hope of returning to her life and job had been squashed.

Ara looked over at Kara and saw a single tear briefly fall from her eye and down her cheek before she quickly brushed it away and regained the perfection required for a New York City receptionist.

Of all the things that Ara thought could have went wrong today, this was not one of them. She'd worried that maybe she would forget what train to take, or that she'd cry when her computer loaded to reveal the image of her and Brad on her Mac desktop monitor. She never in a million years imagined not even making it to her desk. But, apparently, this was the madness she called life lately, laden with one surprise after the other.

"Looks like you may have some free time, Ms. Hopkins," Maro said.

Not knowing a single excusable reason to say no, she agreed to go with the detectives back to the station.

The streets seemed less opportune as each detective walked on either side of her as they exited the building. The buzz that just a few moments ago offered excitement now seemed to be swallowing her whole. Emotionless faces pushed past her without acknowledging that she was obviously having a worse day than your average Starbucks addict.

Ara wanted to kick and scream, really cause a scene and make these men work for their paychecks. But her mother didn't raise her that way. Instead she perched her head firmly on the center of her shoulder blades and looked straight ahead. *What a day to get fired.*

Back at the station in New Jersey, Maro seemed more and more frustrated as Ara sat at the table in the interrogation room without saying a word. Over the past few months, she had mastered locking into her own mind and ignoring her surroundings.

"There are four different prints on the gun. His. Lane Bene's, and yours," he said, "Should we get Detective Bene back in here?"

Ara knew they weren't going to do that. NYPD and Jersey cops competed like a set of twins, two of the same cut from the same gene pool, constantly trying to outdo each other. She almost felt sorry for Detective Maro. He seemed obviously obsessed with the case, proving in her mind that he had no one to go home to.

Earlier on in the investigation, her mother had probed as far as her upper class New Yorker connections allowed her into Detective Maro's life. A social lioness, Arabelle armed herself with the comfort of juicy gossip that could easily be used to her advantage if needed. And juice she'd found. Not only was Detective Maro a miserable two-time failure at marriage, the second one had not only cost him the right to see his children but almost his career. Ara tried, unsuccessfully, to remember the unsavory personal details about Detective Maro her mother had filled her in on. She really should pay attention more when people spoke to her.

"Your husband had a lot of secrets, Ms. Hopkins. More than enough to give you motive," Maro said.

Ara decided to play ball with the fiery detective.

"You've lifted every out of place rock in my life. If he did have secrets, you would know better than me," she said, moving her eyes back to the plain white walls of the interrogation room, painting them with images of her happy place, places that soothed her, wherever those might be.

She knew she was a horrible liar. The very definition of a realist, she could hardly fake her way through high school, let alone entertain the idea of joining a sorority. However, as of late, lying was just another skill she'd unfortunately had the luxury to fine-tune.

"You're right, Ara. I would know. And I do," Maro said. "And what's worse, you know her, too. Actually, you two are quite close."

Ara felt the blood rushing to her face as she rubbed her damp hands back and forth, pulling on each of her left fingers, stopping only for a brief moment to examine her wedding band. "You don't know anything. You just think you do, Detective."

"We'll see about that. Before we let you dig in, a date stuck out to us when reading over these ourselves so we did a little digging. How did you and Brad spend New Year's Eve?"

The room instantly felt blistering hot. That was the day Brad picked her up from the hospital. The forty-eight-hour evaluation she'd received at his suggestion—concerned that she was noticeably feeling down. He didn't know at the time he was sending his pregnant wife in for a pysch evaluation. He was concerned, or so he said, that her depression was coming back.

"I do not want this to get back to the way it was again," he had told her. "You being at your best is most important to me. All I ever want is for you to be happy." *You could have stopped sleeping around,* she thought now. *That would've made me damn happy.*

She'd been reluctant at first but had eventually surrendered since her offices were closed between Christmas and New Year anyway, and quite frankly, she could've used the relaxation.

"Lane told me about a new treatment program at Four Winds out in Westchester. I guess some cops go out there after a trauma. He said it's practically a vacation!" Brad's cheery tone should have made her wonder. He was clearly selling her; why hadn't she seen it?

Snapping her attention back to the detectives she stumbled more than she would have liked to collect her words.

"Brad was concerned, thought I may be getting depressed again. Said that he heard about a place out in Westchester, said it would be like a vacation."

"Why not go on a real vacation, wouldn't that be more typical of a happy husband and wife? Jet off to the Bahamas or choose someplace like it to spend the holiday?"

Ara touched her lip, not knowing what to say. "I think I need my lawyer, Detective."

Maro interrupted, "You were pregnant, and in a facility weeks before your husband was shot dead, clearly you were vulnerable at the time."

"I would like to speak to my lawyer, Barry Goldberg. I'm sure you know the name." Her and Brad's family had friends in high places. And money. A lethal combination in this country. Her mother was right,

98

this was going to be a goddamn circus, and she did need Barry Goldberg, recognized year over year as a winning defense attorney. Ara knew this guy was not someone Maro wanted sitting across the table from him. The way Barry was known to wear down his opposition; it was never death by a single blow. With him, it was death by a thousand paper cuts.

Maro shifted his weight back and forth between each leg and moved a little closer to Ara. Pausing to stare directly into her eyes, he placed a stack of printed out sheets of paper in front of her, tapping the top page. "Here's a little light reading for you. While you wait."

Maro turned on his heel and was out of the interrogation room as quickly as he had picked her up, Ameno following like a sad, attention-seeking puppy.

CHAPTER 14

Sometimes Ara dreamed about the time spent in Dr. Dan's office, though it was hardly a dream, it was just as real as her husband's murder. Three quarters of the doctor's office décor comprised neutral, metallic pallets, while the fourth wall, the one directly behind where he sat to host sessions, exploded with color and mismatched patterns. It was as if he was trying to tell his young patients that they could be whoever they wanted to be in his office. There was no need to hold back, that there was beauty in being different.

After years of insecurities stemming from her parents' expectations of perfection, Ara found the doctor and his crazy decorating habits more than refreshing. He taught her to think freely and injected life back into her.

Little by little, Dr. Dan cracked the shell that Ara had cocooned herself within, exposing the woman Ara desperately wanted to be: confident, beautiful, and happy.

When she was younger, their meetings were much more casual and consisted mostly of Ara playing games on his laptop computer for the length of the overpriced sessions. When Ara would worry that her father, stepmother, or, even worse, her bicoastal mother, would find out about their lack of actual by the book therapy, Dr. Dan would ease all concern promising that their relationship was private, sacred even, like one between lifelong friends. A friendship such as theirs had more much value in life than any sort of therapy he could provide.

It wasn't long after her father died that they started sleeping together, solidifying their freakishly inappropriate bond of an adult doctor and seventeen-year-old patient.

Ara had positioned it just right, setting the tone of their session by confessing to urges she felt she could no longer control. She was testing the grounds of her sexual nature and was exhilarated by it. Dr. Dan had walked over to her side of the office and sat beside her on the leather couch. At first keeping a good foot or so between them, then inching closer and closer, and finally so close she could feel his breath gently at the nape of her neck.

"And what are these feelings you can't ignore?" Dr. Dan had asked, placing one hand on her leg and the other arm behind her, just brushing below her shoulders. Tilting her head to the side, she'd pursed her lips slightly like she saw women in the movies do, and said, "I think you know what they are."

"I'm not so sure that I do know." He retreated slightly, regaining his more professional composure. Suddenly feeling rejected and like she was losing him, Ara reached for his hand and slipped it up her loose-fitting sundress, pressing it hard against herself. "Then I'll show you what I want."

Somewhat shocked by her action, Dr. Dan's professionalism had wilted, revealing a man bulging with want, for her and only her. Before she knew it, he was pressed up against her, forcefully kissing her lips and neck, stealing nibbles here and there all over her body. Ara didn't know what it was that she was feeling, but what she did know was that she had never felt anything like it. It was as if her body was bursting from within. Maybe it was freedom for the very first time, or maybe she had instantly aged ten years. By the time he'd slipped her panties off, she couldn't even fathom what she had started at the beginning of her three o'clock appointment.

"You are absolutely sure, right, Ara?" Dr. Dan had said, gasping for air. But before she could answer, he'd pulled her onto him and began moving her hips up and down.

Was she sure? Moments earlier, she'd known she was. Like most curious, hormone-filled teenagers, she'd dreamed of her first time being perfect. The imperfections of this situation were becoming all too real. Suddenly overtaken by the pain of losing her youth, her confidence diminished and was replaced with childlike disappointment. As she'd watched their reflections in the glass casing of an adjacent bookshelf, she'd hardly recognized the girl straddling her therapist. Despite her being on top, he'd thrusted harder and harder, as if reminding her how very little control she actually had over him.

CHAPTER 15

It was clear what the print outs revealed. Even from afar, Ara could see that the printouts were emails between Brad and Raina's work addresses. *How nice of the detectives to give her her own copy to dissect.* At first she tried to ignore the stack, reiterating to herself that it would only cause her more pain, and that was absolutely not something she thought she could bare. Any married woman who suffered through the torment of a cheating husband could figure out the rest. But curiosity got the best of her.

The all too familiar banter of the unfaithful companions resembled Ara's own courtship with Brad, though she'd obviously lacked Raina's adult film star confidence. Like she needed anything else to make her feel worthless. Why hadn't she ever thought to check on Brad before? It wouldn't have been hard to guess his email password on the apartment desktop; she'd simply have needed to go through all his sports idols, finishing them off with his birthdate. So predictable, in many ways. Or maybe Brad had just been cocky. He had known she would never look. Ara was now convinced it was why he'd married her in the first place.

Adrenaline quickened her breathing as she sifted through his personal conversations. There would be no argument or confrontation. No victory that came with proving he was not holding up his end of the bargain. She would never be able to look at his face as he realized defeat. That she knew everything he thought he'd carefully tied up in technology.

She heard relationships sweep you off your feet but what the fairytales leave out is that after these relationships end, it leaves you gutted, a shell of the person you were before the twister swooped you off to the colorful land of Oz. That returning to black and white is much drearier having experienced the warmth of technicolor.

Ara hated him more and more with each word she read, the pit in her stomach growing. Even feeling sorry for Raina at times, after discovering she wasn't the only one by far. More than once he promised his prospects that his marriage was over, offering subtle details of divorce proceedings she wished she knew about.

Who was this man she had once loved to the core? How could he have had so many secrets?

"You soulless bastard," she whispered aloud. Cursing your dead husband was hardly an absolution.

As she dug deeper and deeper, the worst part were the dates of the interactions, burning her from the inside out. Birthdays, anniversaries, and other various notable holidays shared between them as husband and wife. He'd been fearless, she had to give him that. It seemed he lived more for the thrill than any other inkling of emotion. It certainly was never about love, not even with her.

Why was I such goddamn fool? She'd practically handed her marriage off to these side pieces. Forget having your cake and eating it, too, Brad Bugia had had a personal Viennese table, picking whatever went along with his tastes of the day. One email read:

The past two days were amazing. When you kiss her at midnight, I hope you think of me.

Christ, Ara really hated New Year's Eve. So what she met her husband on the holiday, look how that turned out for her.

There were signs, of course, in the beginning—there always are. Very few relationships take off on a clean runway heading for the crystal blue seas of paradise. Hindsight removes the rose-colored glasses, giving 20/20 cynical vision instead. Brad had occasionally disappeared on "boy's night" benders, only to call begging for Ara's forgiveness at 4 a.m., or sometimes even for her help calling a cab.

Back then she'd made sure she had her fun, too. Guarded by nature, Ara had tried not to disrupt her own pleasures with his insecurities about whether or not he could be a good boyfriend and start his career. But one night, close to their engagement, wrapped in a low count Egyptian cotton sheet, as Dr. Dan was intricately drawing lines up and down her arm, she'd accepted the reality that it would always be about Brad. With Brad, it was always mine, me or I. Leaving no room in their relationship for ours, theirs or you.

Someone less self-absorbed might've realized that while he was belligerently out on the town, the object of his affections was not moping around over a tub of Ben & Jerry's. Ara couldn't see him ever asking what she'd done in his absence.

Maybe he didn't think that much of her. Maybe he should have thought more of her.

Or maybe, things were exactly how they were supposed to be.

It was that night, when she'd realized how self-absorbed Brad truly was, that she'd said goodbye to Dr. Dan for good. Ara knew that she'd either have to accept him how he was or leave him forever, and only she could decide what decision would be better for herself and herself alone. She either had to fully commit to Brad, cut off her own heart's indiscretions, or she'd have to pick Dr. Dan, who had already let her down so many times before. Dan never offered her any long-term stability, so she chose Brad and the life that came with him.

For once, she was going to be the selfish one and think about what was best for her. She closed the door on that chapter with her doctor and lover and readied herself to be the wife of a congressman's son and well-respected Manhattan lawyer. As difficult as it was to leave Dr. Dan, she picked up her dignity and left her youthful blunders behind in his downtown apartment. No one would ever have to know she had a decade-long affair with her therapist, she promised herself that at least.

CHAPTER 16

The detectives weren't gone for five minutes before Dr. Dan frantically dialed Ara over and over, with only seconds between each call attempt. He needed to talk to her to get their story straight. The past they shared was not something he wanted getting out. While he swore at one point in his life he would lose it all for her, now faced with the possibility of losing his license and reputation for sleeping with an underage patient, he was no longer sure she was worth that to him. He wasn't nearly as successful back then when he was starting out and had so much more to lose at this point. If only he had answered his phone that night. What could she possibly have called *him* for?

"Pick up, dammit!" he yelled. His executive assistant, Harley, came running in.

"Did you need something, Doctor? I'm so sorry I didn't hear the first time," she was frantic.

"No, Harley, just a moment of frustration. I have everything I need," he said reassuringly. "Apologies for alerting you." He only stopped her to ask to shut the door behind her, and she was gone.

He picked up the phone again and pressed redial.

He caught a glimpse of the chessboard on his coffee table as the phone rang and rang, and he cursed the snarky detectives who'd brushed past it, knocking the two rooks, a few pawns, and her highness to the floor. *Assholes, barging in here like that!* All over a Facebook message, how could he be so stupid?

No answer, again. Frustrated, he slammed down his phone.

Dr. Dan never felt uncomfortable, but those bastard detectives had really ground at his confidence. Detectives Maro and Ameno hadn't been as much suspicious as they'd been expectant. Completely upfront about how they were going to get over on him. Sitting back obnoxiously, patient, knowing he had a story to tell, and they were going to count the sweat beads accumulating at his hairline until he told it.

"So you treated Ms. Hopkins throughout her mid-to-late teen years, Dr. DaVedere?" Ameno had said. "What was the basis of these sessions? Normal angst from puberty or did you suspect deeper issues?"

Wetting his lips, Dr. Dan said, "First off, as I am sure you are aware, I am bound to patient and doctor confidentiality. Unless you have a warrant?" The detectives shook their heads no. "Didn't think so.

However, I am happy to help. Ara was always very special but at times could be her own worst enemy. The world was a bit too rough for her, shall we say. She was always very sensitive. You know I can't go much further than that."

"Sounds like you really cared for the girl," Maro had said with a look of disgust.

"I care for all of my patients, Detective. I'm sure you could understand; I am very passionate about my work." Did she tell them something or could they just see right through him?

"How did the Hopkins family find you to seek treatment for Ara?" The younger detective was much calmer.

"I don't recall. It was quite a while ago," Dr. Dan said. "Detectives, I haven't treated Ara in years, but I'm still bound by patient confidentiality. I'm not entirely sure how I could be of help to you here."

Silence filled the gap as Dr. Dan had stood, hoping they would take the hint that the conversation was over.

"We saw a comment on a Facebook photo that seemed to indicate you were really trying to reach out to her," Maro said.

Dr. Dan smiled. "Social media. . . it has eroded our culture. But yes, I was concerned for her. Dealing with a sudden death of a loved one can really pommel one's psyche."

"Why use Facebook? I would expect you have her telephone number," Ameno said. The doctor's lips pulled together in a tight crease.

"True, very true. Her cell phone went straight to voicemail. I'm assuming with the death of her husband and," he paused, "law enforcement trying to shift the focus onto her and her private matters, she is not taking that many calls at the moment."

Maro scoffed, "We consider all valid leads, Doctor, being that we are *passionate* about our jobs and all."

That's when Dr. Dan had pressed the button on his desk signaling Harley to come in with a fake emergency with a patient, a ploy which had saved him more than once.

Within seconds, the door opened and Harley had floated in to share her fake tale. "Doctor, a patient has been taken back into the hospital. Another suicide attempt, the mother is hysterical." She was a great actress. *Should've stuck with it,* he'd thought.

"Of course. Harley, pull the file and I'll be done in a moment," he said. "Gentleman?" The detectives stood, ignoring the gesture of his outstretched hand.

"We'll be in touch," Ameno said as the two left the office. Maro had bumped the table, sending the chess pieces scrambling to the floor. "Hope it wasn't a good game." And they were gone.

Since the first time Ara spoke of him, he knew Brad Bugia and his family would cause trouble. He didn't think Brad would end up dead, but he always feared the effect dating such a high-profile person would have on Ara's life. He had cautioned her from getting involved with a family like that. He knew that cocky bastard would screw them both one day. But little by little, he could tell she was falling for him, trusting Brad more and more as things were getting serious. That was when he started watching the couple, to keep Ara safe. At least, that was his reasoning at first. But then he started following Brad alone and before long he was following him and Raina as they slunk between late night spots and seedier hotels well below Brad's typical budget.

Night after night in dimly lit corners of uptown bars, he tightened his grip around his twenty-year-old scotch, partly from anger and partly with a drop of hope. Brad had the one thing he'd always wanted, yet was

willing to toss it aside for a piece of promiscuous trash. It bothered him,

deep inside, that the universe could be this unfair. And how could Brad

subject *his* perfect Ara to such cruelty? Innocence was always one of her

most endearing qualities, like a bright light in this world that refused to

be diminished, but how could she be so naïve not to see something so

brash happening right under her nose? Not him. He had always seen

Brad for exactly who he was. And he despised every bit of him. Brad

Bugia would not bring him or Ara down. He would make sure of it.

CHAPTER 17

"What are you ordering?" Raina asked. The two women sat across from each other at one of their favorite Manhattan brunch spots. Nothing better than bottomless mimosas and some modern twist on eggs benedict chock full of avocado and kale.

"I'm not really that hungry," Ara replied. "Probably just mimosas for me." She could hardly stomach the site of Raina knowing what she knew now, let alone food.

Raina's displeasure peeked over the top of her oversized sunglasses. Ara sensed her alarm and rolled her eyes.

"OK, fine, I'll get a spinach and goat cheese omelet," Ara said just to ease the building tension.

A stumpy waitress greeted the duo, taking their order, suggesting they go for the bottomless mimosas if they planned on having more than two. Which, of course, they did. Within minutes a bottle of champagne sat perched on ice next to the table and they were about halfway through the first round.

They chit-chatted over insignificant topics, until even those started to run dry. Ara remembered a time when their relationship didn't seem as forced. Back to a time where they almost cared for each other, and spent countless hours cuddled up on one another's dorm room beds planning their futures, or the takedown of a competing ex-girlfriend. There was a livelihood to their partnership that had been broken. And each girl blamed the other. Their food arrived, which provided a good break from the meaningless banter that was getting more difficult by the minute.

"I can't believe I'm thirty-one," Raina sighed. Ara knew she was extremely bothered by another year of her life flying by without even the slightest prospect of a husband.

"It's not so bad," Ara said. "Age is just a number. Plus, you still look like you're twenty-five, so that's a plus." Up until a moment ago, Ara actually forgot they were even out celebrating her birthday. "And hey, I'm alone now, too, so at least you got what you wanted there." Before she even finished the sentence, Ara knew she had opened a door she was not willing to fully walk through.

"What's that supposed to mean, Ar?" Raina said, her glance now firmly focused on Ara, even through her sunglasses.

"I didn't mean anything by it. I just know that you always missed when it was just me and you, that's all." Why did she have to slip up and say anything?

"Sure, but I certainly don't think I preferred your husband dead. How could you even imply something like that?"

"You never wanted me and Brad to end up all married with children, and you know it. I'm not implying anything other than that now you have nothing to be jealous of. I'm a widow, which is so much worse than being single, and half the country thinks I'm a psycho murdering bitch, so you're better off than me right now. That is all I'm saying." She really should have stopped at her fourth mimosa.

Raina's lips turned down with anger as she violently sliced through her French toast, taking a large bite before saying, "You *would* need a reason to blame this all on me, wouldn't you? God forbid you messed it up on your own without your slutty, hot mess evil stepsister to blame."

"Raina, you are overreacting, and I'm not in the mood. Can we just forget I said it? I didn't mean anything by it, I'm probably just drunk from all of the mimosas on an empty stomach."

"Maybe that's the problem, you're never in the mood! Too wrapped up in your own pathetic world," Raina shouted, French toast spitting from her mouth. Other brunchers, who would never dream of causing a scene, looked on as if it were a reality show. "You think we all have to fall all over you now because you lost Brad, but you did this to yourself. You are one hundred percent to blame."

"You can't possibly be blaming me for Brad's death, that's ridiculous," Ara spat, ignoring her instinct to keep quiet in public.

"No, but I am blaming you for this pathetic pity party and making something that is hard for everyone all about you."

Ara's hand shook, clattering her knife against the plate as she sliced through her omelet. "He was *my* husband. Not yours. You would think it would be a little more about me."

"Maybe so, but this hasn't exactly been easy on anyone."

"I know, Raina," was all Ara said. How she wished she could have confronted her in front of the perfectly dressed brunchers on her role in their marriage falling apart.

"You don't know shit." Pushing back her chair, Raina stormed from the table with her usual dramatics.

I know everything, Ara thought as the eyes of the other guests condemned her from all angles.

CHAPTER 18

Ara couldn't remember the exact moment her marriage fell apart. To be honest, up until her husband's blood redecorated their living room walls, she'd thought she was happy. God, marriage to a politician's son had seemed so much better on the big screen. Brad was calculated, but she'd loved that about him. After two weeks in Grenada for their honeymoon, she'd accepted the reality that neither one of them would ever truly relax. While other couples perched themselves on lounge chairs, tangled up in newly-wedded bliss, Ara resembled more of an animal who needed to be fed, pathetically two steps behind Brad as he waltzed through the upscale resort, joining beach volleyball games with strangers, water polo matches, and poker tournaments. Introducing himself to one upper crust couple after the next, solidifying quite a few contacts he'd follow up with once back in New York. His digital rolodex bursting at the seams with new acquaintances, all at the expense of his new marriage. They would always have time for each other, he'd say, a lifetime. Ara couldn't help now but to laugh at his arrogance; his lifetime hadn't ended up being that long.

Their anniversary trip the next year followed suit. She'd stood beachside, eyes scanning the seemingly endless sea, her right hand offering limited shade from the glare. Looking out past the jetty to the specks sashaying back and forth across the waters on their jet skis and paddle boards. Brad would head out for hours, leaving her on shore by herself.

At least down there in the sun, where she was his only option, they made love as much as she pleased. She wanted to be a mother, and their sex life at home was already dissipating to nonexistent. They had exhausted the topic, whole-heartedly complete with a few pros and con lists and excel spreadsheets of the financial aspect. Brad usually ended the conversation with some jab that they both knew she couldn't give up wine for nine months anyway. It was easier than saying what he really meant, he didn't want to start a family with her.

This last trip, however, Ara was prepared. Bringing all the bells and whistles Brad enjoyed, floss-like lingerie and a few items on the conservative end of S&M props. Their sex life was passionate, and occasionally crossed the line to straight kinky, but never to the point where a safe word was necessary. Ara kept his interest as she strapped herself into an outfit she had ordered from some lingerie-of-the-month club, tapping him lightly on his bare skin with her whip. Within seconds, he'd risen to his knees revealing his now-hardened penis, obviously pleased with the shakeup. Ara slapped his forearm as he reached for her. "No, no, bad boy. No touching," she'd said, fueling his already-heightened drive. Ara backed him up to the bed and spread his arms and legs to the four post banisters, securing each with a soft length of fabric. Loose enough that Brad could probably escape at any time but tight enough to drive the excitement. She crawled up his lower half before turning her back to him, easing herself down to take him in reverse cowgirl since Brad always called himself an "ass man" as vulgar as that sounded. Moaning, she finished him off, falling back onto the pillows and her favorite spot in Brad's shoulder.

"I saw that on Nickelodeon once and always wanted to try it," Brad said as they both burst into laughter. "You're confusing *Fifty Shades of Grey* and *Titanic*," she'd said, unable to control herself. Naturally his response included the idea of making a porno.

"Why don't you teach me how to play chess downstairs instead?" she proposed, confident he would take the bait. This wouldn't be their first attempt. What often started in jest over a bottle of red, usually concluded with Ara insisting Brad was speaking to her like a zoo animal. He wasn't nearly as patient with her as Dan, who taught her to play years ago. It was easier to act like she needed teaching than to actually beat Brad. It would take days for him to recover from his wounded ego, and that was a trouble she didn't need to deal with. Back at home in New Jersey, the two would sit across from each other at Brad's antique chess table like a couple of old English schoolmates catching up. The table, a wedding gift from his grandfather, was one of the few belongings Ara ever saw Brad express any emotion over. Unlike most men, he never hung onto old sports team's T-shirts or foul balls, but Brad's grandfather was a man of great stature, and having his chess table in their living room made Brad feel important.

"Maybe the Caribbean air will bring you luck," Brad said as he jumped from the bed. Ara was hoping it would, too; her chance of getting pregnant was riding on this trip.

They strolled through the lobby hand-in-hand and out to the breezy, covered piazza where the hotel had a chess board set up adjacent to the bar. They ordered a bottle of cheap champagne, the kind they wouldn't be caught dead drinking back home. But on an island resort, miles away from New York, anything with a recognizable brand name was welcomed.

Ara took a long draft, finishing her glass in a single tilt, nodding for a replacement before the waitress left.

As he set up the board, Brad walked through the pieces and rules of the game as he had many times before.

"This piece, they call it a rook," Brad said, swirling the piece in his hand like a fine wine. "It's a misunderstood and often misused piece."

"How so?" Ara asked, faking interest as she took another sip, lingering on the tartness of the champagne's price point.

"Rooks need to be paired with each other or another piece to have power." The drama in his tone was derisive. "You see, they start in the corners of the board and can only move forward and back, so they can't really do all that much and don't seem like a threat."

Ara wanted to yell as Brad moved his hands in the motion over the board. She enjoyed learning to play chess from Dr. Dan, who, unlike Brad, had never made her feel like she didn't have two brain cells to rub together. Dan was quite the wordsmith, everything he'd said at the time, came off as a compliment.

You don't want a rook castling with the king, Dr. Dan had once told her. *Think of it like shacking up. When a rook and a king are in this position they support one another and the rook can move easier around the board toward more favorable positions.*

Back in the Caribbean, Ara said, "The queen is still the strongest in the game, right?" as she mimicked a royal stance and a fake crown on her head. Brad laughed, reaching across the table and pulling her in, kissing the top of her head where her pretend crown would've sat.

"Yes, that is true. But," he said, "don't be overconfident, your highness. Even a queen may be sacrificed for a more fortunate position."

"So you're saying even a queen can get rooked."

Brad laughed. "Look at you and your clever word choice. Chess is a lot like life, Ara, anyone can have anything taken from them at any time, and yes, anyone can get screwed."

Their eyes locked as he finally took a sip of his champagne. She looked toward the blue water and said, "Good to know," before tipping her head, chugging the rest of her champagne, and signaling for another

from the bar.

CHAPTER 19

Standing up from the table, Ara signed the check, tucking her

mother's credit card back in her wallet. It was just like Raina to walk out

without paying her share of the bill. Rubbing her temples, she realized

the bottomless mimosas had had more of an effect on her than she'd

originally thought. It was barely 4 p.m., and she was as drunk as an

underage sorority sister after a night of hard-core initiation partying. Ara

made her way to the busy street, fumbling with her cell phone. Thinking

she should take an Uber, she struggled trying to drop the pin in her exact

location. She was about two years behind the rest of her generation in

learning new technology, something she often laughed about

considering her past career in digital advertising. Her complete lack of

capabilities when it came to technology amused Brad, who was a natural

whiz. "You are a bad millennial," he had joked after she found herself

cruising down the Garden State Parkway toward the Jersey Shore

instead of their waterfront Jersey City apartment. She had whined the

whole way back to the city about how it was ridiculous that the app made you drop the pin in your exact location as Brad continued on about millennials needing everything to be effortless.

Only two years older, his superior ways could be quite irritating. His natural smugness and hate for living on the other side of the river was hard to ignore. "No one dreams of being bridge and tunnel," he'd say before moving on to his father's help. "My father can help us close the gaps, fill in if we need it for the security deposit or something. He'd want us in Manhattan."

Ara would cringe every time he said the word, *Manhattan,* arguing that he should call it New York, or The City, or anything other than *Manhattan.*

"That is what it is called babe. Man-hattan. We would never have to leave, we'd have it all," he would promise.

She'd scrunch her nose at his pretentious tone as his nose seemed to lift a little more to the sky. To Brad, they were on their way to being untouchable. Nothing was going to stop him from getting to the top.

Ara, on the other hand, loved their Newport address. Many nights as Brad attended happy hours and dinners, she'd look out their ten foot windows at the bright city lights, enlivened with power. From her view, she felt she could see everything.

"Ara Hopkins," said a familiar voice. "You look like you are having yourself a fine weekend stroll."

Ara looked up and saw the second-to-last person she wanted to see while drunk on a sidewalk in the middle of the afternoon. Detective Jason Ameno walked toward her, extending his right hand. At least it wasn't Detective Maro. She didn't think she could spar with the "bad cop" of the pair on the amount of alcohol she'd consumed.

"Hello, Detective," Ara said, loosely putting her hand in his. "What are you doing in the city?" Ara knew it was a silly question; obviously he was here because of her.

"Just brunching with friends," he said, but by the looks of his standard detective ensemble—striped shirt, loose-fitting tie, and outlet dress pants—she could more than assume that wasn't the case. Spinning just a little too fast to walk in the opposite direction, Ara's heel got caught in a crack in the sidewalk and sent her tumbling to the ground. Now shaken, she fumbled to pick up the loose items from her purse as Detective Ameno gently kicked a rolling Chanel lipstick in her direction.

"Too much fun today at your own brunch, Ms. Hopkins," he said in a way that lacked any resemblance of a question.

"Because I'm the only widow to get trashed before 4 p.m.?" Ara said, pulling her skirt back to cover her as she rose from the pavement. She tried to come up with a hard-hitting insult but was instead left mouth open, searching for words to fill the gaps.

"Of course not, Ms. Hopkins," he said, gently placing an arm around her waist. Leaning in close enough for her to smell the recent cigarette he'd smoked. "Self-medicating, are we?"

"Why can't you just leave me alone?" she said as she pushed him. "This is fun for you, isn't it? Isn't it!"

Detective Ameno wasted no time. "No, Ara, it is not fun for me. Sure, I came to talk to you but now you are visibly intoxicated, yelling on a street." Huffing he continued, "Can I at least give you a ride home or call someone for you?" He didn't wait for an answer and began walking her toward the rear passenger side door of his undercover car.

After helping her in, Ameno slammed the door and walked around the trunk of the car where he kicked at the gravel, toddler like, before getting in the front seat.

"Let me be straight with you, Ms. Hopkins," he said. "Your husband was a dirt bag. He had other women, shady friends, poor business dealings, he had it all. Some would say he even deserved it. But I need you to help me here. The pressure at the department and with Maro . . . ." he trailed off, obviously contemplating if he said too much already.

Maro couldn't be easy to work with, Ara thought, suddenly feeling the slightest ping of compassion for Ameno. "Arrest me, please, so I can call my lawyer." They both knew he wasn't going to do that, he had no reason and he sure as hell wasn't going to take any chances. Not on a high-profile case like this and not when she had Barry Goldberg on retainer.

Ara's drunken eyes flooded. *Your husband was a dirt bag*. The phrase seemed like the type of thing only she was allowed to say. Brad was her self-centered jerk to call names. Not some detective looking to make a jump in his career off of her failed marriage and obvious lack of ability to judge a person's character. But he was right, Brad really was a dirt bag. A self-centered, weak man, who'd thought only of himself.

"Why are you following me, Detective? Is it protocol to stalk your suspects?" Ara's mind raced through every crime show she ever indulged in, trying decide if this was a normal situation. "Let's be straight. You want me to confess to murder so you can outshine your partner and become the hero cop who sweet-talked me into a confession. Am I getting this right?" The champagne started to turn on her as her right temple began to throb. Leaning back against the leather, she sighed. "You think very little of me, Detective, don't you?"

Ameno fumbled with a few knobs up front, presumably checking that his radio was off before saying, "That's not true at all. I think quite a bit of you actually."

"Oh yeah?" Ara said, more eagerly than she would have liked. *Damn you, champagne.*

"Slow your roll." *Caught.* "Either you are a brilliant black widow who is managing to get away with her husband's murder, or you yourself are a victim, and someone may want to hurt you. Either way, that makes you a person of interest to me," Ameno said before continuing, "and the ID Network, eventually, I'm sure, for a weekend special."

132

"You wouldn't believe me even if I told you the truth," she said.

"Try me."

"I knew everything about Brad," Ara began, only to be interrupted by Ameno's thoughtless laughter. For someone who was trying to cohere a confession out of her, he certainly lacked any sort of swagger. "I knew he was unfaithful. I just didn't—" hesitating only to press the record button on her voice memo app to safe guard herself"—I didn't know every last steamy detail. But I knew he was having affairs."

Ara was shocked she thought to record the conversation, but she'd been married to a lawyer, after all. Brad barely ordered lunch without recording the evidence. Though now she knew there was plenty in his life he didn't want a record of.

"I know how it all works, Detective. You don't get to where Brad was by playing by the rules," she said dryly, hoping the champagne was at least assisting her acting abilities. She needed an infusion of Brad's smooth confidence.

"You were OK with that, Ms. Hopkins?" Ameno asked. "To think you were starting a family with this man."

"Accepting, I suppose." An honest answer. "Sometimes your judgment is clouded by the things that you want in life." *Sometimes it seems so much harder to start over*, Ara finished silently in her head. This may be the part of the truth that she was not ready to admit openly to others. "What I'm trying to say, Detective, is I had come to terms with certain aspects of my life, because I was looking forward to so many other things. My dreams died with Brad that night."

An understanding, disguised in a comforting silence, sat right between the two.

"If it makes you feel better, I am not interested in you as the suspect," Ameno said matter-of-factly. "Maro is the one with the hard-on. I just think you know more than you're letting on."

"I've just learned to not let my emotions get the best of me."

Ameno grunted. "You may use your phone, call your own ride home. Of course, that may alter your recording," he said with a glance in the rear-view mirror that could be mistaken as charming.

"Detective Bene is already on his way," Ara said as she returned the glance.

"Of course he is. When did you text him?"

"Right before I got in the car."

Lane pulled up just a few moments later and rushed toward them, looking ready for an altercation as he knocked forcefully on the driver side window. Ameno shimmied out of the seat.

"Calm down, Bene. All is good," Ameno said, acting more like a fraternity brother whose house party got busted than a detective. "No trouble for Ms. Hopkins, just wanted to make sure she got home safely."

Lane scoffed. "Back off Ara, Ameno, before there's a harassment charge smacked on your desk."

Ameno shifted his weight and leaned in toward Lane. "I said there was no problem, Bene." He opened the rear driver's side door, allowing Ara to step from the car. Lane reached for her hand and walked her back around the car and to the sidewalk.

"I think a judge would be more interested in your emotional involvement, Bene. Banging the victim's widow is usually frowned upon in an open case."

Lane rushed back toward Ameno threateningly. "I said back off, Detective."

Though slightly amused by the situation, Ara did not need this ending up on social media or worse the news. She yelled, "It's my fault, Lane, let's just go home."

"You're being summoned," Ameno smirked, taking a few steps back to the driver side of the car. Lane once again took Ara's hand, pausing only to point at Ameno, "Leave her alone, Detective."

Once in Lane's passenger seat, Ara was happy to be alone with him. She preferred this cop and his car over her earlier company. Lane brought a calmness to her even though she knew him well enough to know that he was angry and that his repeated comments about getting foolishly drunk in the afternoon came from a place of genuine concern.

It's not that Lane was wrong. She should be keeping a low profile, not get obliterated in public mid-day. The media was probably wishing her story would turn into a *Dateline*-type tale featuring both Brad and her own glamorous upbringings as the fortunate offspring of the tristate area's one percent: each provided every opportunity the competitive city and its sprawling suburbs bursting with country clubs and overpriced mansions had to offer. The truth was in the lies that were concealed behind the prettiest of packaging.

I should pitch this, Ara thought, chuckling. At least the world would get the chance to see Brad without his expert wrapping and pretty little bow.

"You are really something," Lane said, interrupting her thought. "And who the hell is Danielle? I don't ever remember you mentioning someone by that name, but she was calling you like crazy this morning."

Dammit, Dr. Dan, Ara thought. She didn't realize Lane had picked up on her ignoring the calls.

"An old friend, Lane, nothing to worry about. She's probably just concerned."

"Some friend, I feel like she called ten times before noon. A few more calls and I would think she was some kind of stalker or something."

Ara's stomach turned; she didn't need him finding anything on her sordid past. "I told you, it's an old friend. Next time, don't pretend to be sleeping if it's bothering you."

"Well, be careful. I'm just trying to keep you out of trouble. It's amazing the people that come out of the weeds when you're going through something." Lane slammed his blinker knob and made a quick left in the opposite direction of Ara's apartment.

"Danielle is nothing to worry about." Holding her phone to the right of her crossed leg, she edited contact *Danielle* to now read *Lady Dr.* "Deleted." She held up the phone to Lane. "See. Problem solved. So, can we please forget it and move on?"

"You didn't have to do that," Lane said, "I was just wondering."

"Don't you think if I wanted to talk to her, I would?"

Lane only nodded and Ara hoped it was enough of an explanation to keep him from asking any more about Dr. Dan and his disguised alias in her cell phone.

CHAPTER 20

"Jesus, Hernandez." Detective Ben Maro massaged his fevered brow as pain intensified behind his eyelids. "It doesn't need to be reassigned. I'm close. We are just about to solve this thing, you have to believe me. Where the hell is Jason?"

"I'm not going to reassign the case, but I've heard it before, Detective. And it's not that I don't trust you." The DA hesitated before adding, "It's just that this needs to be neat and clean. I think your tunnel vision has gotten the best of you."

Pushing back folders stuffed full with papers and a few Dunkin Donuts cups, Maro shoved a file against Martina Hernandez's chest. "Tunnel vision, eh? For Christ's sake, gimme more credit than that," he said before storming off to call his partner.

"Please tell me you have something from today," he practically yelled into the phone.

"Nothing. I tried catching her off guard, hoped after the booze she'd talk more but she called Bene before I could have a decent conversation. He said to back off, Maro, got a little heated."

"So let me guess, you backed off and got nothing?" Maro didn't need to hear the answer, he knew Ameno was too busy playing by the rules. Just two years older than Brad Bugia, he was a charismatic cop and determined politician himself, easily climbing his way from parking tickets to a rising detective. With a sergeant position opening a few Septembers from now, Maro knew Ameno more than hoped this case would prove to be his golden ticket. Problem was, Ameno didn't think Ara was the killer.

"I wouldn't say nothing. Bene, he didn't take Ara home. They both went into his building looking every bit like a couple."

"What do you mean like a couple?"

"You know, holding hands like they're in a relationship or something. Don't you think it's weird he seems to show up just in time, every time? That night even, how did he get to the Bugia apartment so fast?"

Maro considered what his partner was presenting. Lane Bene had been adamant on Ara's innocence but could his detective eye be obstructed by his lust for her? Maro had to agree that there was something about Ara Hopkins that seemed mysterious, appealing even.

140

Like she was a little bird whose safety and honor was every man's responsibility to protect. She was vulnerable in the sexiest of ways and completely unaware of her effect on people. Or, did Lane have a thing for his best friend's girl? His prints were on the gun. So were others, so that alone wasn't enough. Any decent defense attorney would argue that as a trained professional, he was simply showing his friend how to use the weapon. And that the romantic affair he was now involved in was nothing more than a friend comforting a friend during a tragedy that grew into something more.

"You may be onto something. Let's look into their relationship," Maro said.

They needed to find something that could link someone — anyone, though he'd prefer it was Ara or Lane — to Brad's death. They had one problem, Brad Bugia's lifestyle resembled one of a Hollywood actor. No one hated him. Women flocked to him, screwed him, and left him on their own accord wearing a newfound confidence in place of a diamond ring or fancy gift for silence. Colleagues respected him, even lawyers twenty years his senior. Clients who kept him on retainer, and those in his father's circle, looked up to him. Through his investigation he gathered that Brad was trusted not only by those he protected under the law, but also by those closest to the Democratic party to collect funds for their campaigns. Conveniently, most of his clients were donors, and it seemed Brad was the link. Problem was, as far as Maro could see, there wasn't a person on this island who wasn't enamored by him. He may have had some fancy friends, but everything, professionally at least, seemed mostly by the books.

But men like that just didn't get targeted for no reason. It couldn't have been a random act. Someone thought long and hard about the up and comer and someone wanted to permanently pause his parade and Maro desperately needed to figure out who this person was.

CHAPTER 21

Raina hurried across town, troubled by the sensation that she was being followed. Was she losing her mind? Of course, there were perverts and predators, but in the early evening, one could usually assume most New Yorkers were more concerned with meeting friends at the next drinks spot or getting the last bike in a soul cycle class.

Raina stopped suddenly, turning on her left heel and tightly gripping a corkscrew she had in her Michael Kors crossover bag. A man in his early twenties, the double brunching type, slammed into her, yelping as the corkscrew nicked his shoulder.

"What the hell, you crazy bitch!" he shouted, now drawing the attention of the phone-yielding army. "Did you stab me?" For once, Raina was speechless as she shoved the opener back into her bag. "I am so sorry," she said, tilting her head a bit flirtatiously and regaining her composure, hoping to ease his anger over the nick in his arm.

"You think I would find you attractive after you stab me?" He laughed, pushing her down to the sour pavement. "Pathetic." He stepped over her, regarding her more as a piece of trash than a woman he just shoved to the ground in front of countless witnesses.

Six or so socially sick individuals held their cameras in focus instead of offering her a helping hand. This day was really starting to get the best of her. Just before she burst into an embarrassing flood of pity tears, a thirtysomething man slipped through the crowd and swooped her to her feet.

"Nothing to look at here, move along," he said to the pedestrians. "You OK?" The crowd mumbled and put their phones down and continued along with their days, unfazed.

Although not usually keen on crying in front of random good-looking men, Raina let out what seemed to be months of overdue tears into the man's blazer. He rubbed her back, whispering, "Don't worry, I'm a doctor. Is everything OK? Do you want me to take you somewhere or call someone?"

Four hours and three dirty martinis later, Raina was half dressed in the doctor's Upper East Side apartment. They'd barely made it in the front door before Raina's skirt was pushed up and her shirt pulled over her head. Despite the haste to get down to things, the doctor more than

144

held his own as they passionately moved through the apartment, finishing on the floor sprawled out in front of his large unlit fireplace and sixty-inch TV. He pulled a blanket down from the chaise lounge to cover their bottom halves and clicked on the classic rock music channel with the remote before placing it back on the coffee table.

"Wine?" he asked. Since Raina rarely turned down what she was sure would be an expensive bottle, she agreed. "Stay here," he said. "Relax." He returned a few moments later with two wine glasses and an uncorked bottle.

"I figured I should do the opening, you look pretty dangerous with a corkscrew."

She couldn't help but laugh. "Thank you for helping me today," she said. "I'm usually not such a crazy person. Just dealing with a difficult situation." Raina hoped he wouldn't press for too much more out of respect for her distinct elusiveness. Her relationship with Ara was complicated enough but the current state of it was difficult to understand without sharing that she had sex, for years, with her stepsister's husband. And worse, that she allowed herself to fall in love with him.

If she could have only known when she introduced the two that it would forever impact her sanity, causing the next five years to be practically unbearable. Living with regret was not something Raina enjoyed, but in this situation, she was confident the outcome could have been different had she put her mind and, of course, body to it.

If only Raina had had her future goggles strapped on a little tighter that night she would have never passed off Brad to her dull Ara that night. Brad was the better long-term match for Raina and like an idiot she handed him right over to her stepsister, like she needed another reason to be jealous of her. But at the time, Brad had just graduated from law school and was not yet the rising star that he was the day of his death. Ara had loved him as he'd worked his way up, and not just because who his father was, which Raina knew Brad respected. But if it had meant everything to him, she would not have been able to persuade him into an affair as easily as she had. Brad Bugia had been looking for an escape from his cookie-cutter life, and it had barely taken the promise of a blow job to move his attention elsewhere.

"I'm sorry to hear you're having a bad day." Raina's attention snapped back to her current lover, pausing only slightly at the thought that he, too, seemed to be a good catch.

"Well, they tend to happen to the best of us," she said. "Nothing I can't get over."

The doctor moved to stand, pulling her to her feet. Maneuvering behind her, he began to massage her shoulders, working his hands to the base of her neck and then down her spine. He pressed up against her, moving his hands around her waist, and walked her to the bedroom.

What a relief, Raina thought, *a man who doesn't pry.*

Despite the high-count Egyptian cotton sheets and the warmth of the doctor lying next to her, Raina couldn't sleep or shake the uneasiness that threatened her sense of peace. Slipping out from under the sheets trying not to disturb her bed partner, she rummaged on the floor for her purse before snagging it and slipping out to the living room. Shivering, Raina wrapped a throw blanket around her from the sofa and retrieved Detective Maro's card from her wallet. She typed in the number as she walked toward the front door entrance, away from the bedroom so the doctor wouldn't hear.

After a few rings, she said, "I'm sorry to wake you. Oh good, I can't sleep either. There's something I need to tell you about Ara I think you should know."

CHAPTER 22

Ara for once woke peacefully on Lane's couch, propped up against an oversized throw pillow. Knowing Lane's lack of regard for decorating, she was certain his mother or an ex-girlfriend had purchased it for him. Squinting at the time flashing on the cable box she sat up and scanned the room, panicking only slightly when she couldn't locate her phone and laughing at herself for how naked and exposed she felt without it.

"Looking for something?" Lane said, shaking the phone about head high with more than a touch of sarcasm. "You're quite popular this morning, you got a ton of messages this morning, now your doctor is texting you like crazy, is everything OK?"

Thrown slightly by the question, she reached up to grab the phone as Lane held it higher above his head, wishing she had turned off her lock screen notifications. He then placed his left hand on her lower belly, feeling right through to where Brad's baby had once been. "I didn't think anything of it at first, and I wouldn't have pried but then I thought it may be serious."

Her brain scrambled to put the blurry pieces together from her day drinking day gone wrong. *God, she needed to stop drinking so much alcohol*, she thought. It did not take long before she remembered a switch she made to her contacts last night. "First question Mr. Bene, how did you guess my passcode? But more importantly did the doctor get back to me? I texted the office the other day."

She could only hope Dr. Dan had kept it professional in his correspondence, it was a scenario they had discussed at length for years. Whatever he needed, if he was going to contact her, his composure had to remain intact.

"Well, Ms. Hopkins, you told it to me a few days ago," Lane said, jokingly tapping the tip of her nose. "I didn't know doctor offices texted with their patients these days. Is that common?"

"I think I'm somewhat of a special circumstance. With everything going on, they know I like to interact with the least number of people as possible." Ara brushed the loose hair back off her shoulders and smiled up at Lane, who was still holding her phone out of reach. "May I have my phone back please? I'm fine, I promise."

Lane searched her face, looking for any indication of dishonesty probably, before handing the phone over to her. "They just said to stop in the office if at all possible this morning. Sure it's nothing serious?"

Scrolling through the texts in her log, she opened Dan's, hoping she'd at least been smart enough to delete their previous texts. *Phew!* She was getting better at thinking ahead.

Lane brushed her cheek, giving it a peck before heading back to the kitchen where he had breakfast fit for an entire high school football team laid out on the table.

Happy for the chance to change the subject, Ara said, "Are you expecting someone other than us?"

Looking down at the table, his arms stretched out over two different chairs, he said, "Nope, I was just having a hard time guessing what you wanted."

"Eggs are fine." Lane looked displeased at her lack of enthusiasm toward his gesture, so she continued, "And who doesn't love bacon." He pulled back the chair to his right and mocking an uptown waiter said, "Madam" as he overly exaggerated a wave for her to sit.

Instead she wrapped both of her arms loosely around his waist. As their lips touched, she could feel the tension leave his body.

CHAPTER 23

Dr. Dan's eyes flew open, sprung awake by his own feelings of an imminent threat. He could hear Raina on the phone out in the hall and hearing what he was now, he may have to act sooner than he thought. He needed to keep her close, that's why he spent the time following her and suffered through an entire evening without strangling her. He needed to know what she was up to. For Ara's sake. But for now, he couldn't let on that he knew who she was. He had to play it cool and keep up the charade as hard as that would be. He closed his eyes again and begged for sleep to come quickly.

At 9 a.m., a text message alert shook him awake. He went to the bathroom, locked the door behind him, and tore off his T-shirt, his heart racing with the ups and downs of the past twenty-four hours. Nothing calmed him like a warm shower. At times, it was the only place he could actually think for himself. It was an odd thing, making a living from working through others' emotions. Of course, the industry lingo framed it up all pretty in a "helping others" package, but what it often left out was the power a doctor in his field so often had over his patients. Yes, good doctors could guide those struggling with mental health issues down the correct path, and almost like another parent, bear witness to the person's life, offering assistance and alternative perspectives when needed. But the responsibility that came with that was huge and, more often than not, could be depressively overwhelming.

His phone buzzed on the vanity. He quickly rinsed the Old Spice body wash from his face and reached for his towel, covering himself before he typed the pass code into his phone.

I can be in at 11am, read the text. "Perfect," he said out loud.

"Everything OK? Can I come in?" Raina called into the bathroom as she knocked on the door. He had to get rid of her. He would deal with her eventually, of course, but right now he needed to speak with Ara.

He unlocked the door and opened it to find Raina inches away. "Yes, fine, I need to go into the office, sorry to rush you out," he said, brushing past her toward his armoire. As he fished through his shirts, he noticed she was not moving. *This chick is unyielding.*

"I have to go to work," he repeated. "Sorry to rush you, but the whole day kind of got away from me yesterday. I have appointments today that I would hate to reschedule."

Raina moved toward him and buttoned the top two buttons on his Simon Miller shirt. "No worries, it was fun," she said, standing on the tips of her toes to give him a kiss. Reluctantly kissing her back, his hands moved to below her waist. Raina took her lips to his chest and began to make her way south before he interrupted, "I'd love to see you again, but really, I need to go."

"Sure thing," she said, rolling her eyes. "I'll grab my things."

"Can I get you a car or something to get home?" he asked.

"No, no, I can make my own way, thank you."

Dr. Dan grabbed his wallet from a nearby table and began to make his way to the front door. "Feel free to take your time, just lock the door behind you on your way out."

He thought he heard Raina say something in response but didn't turn back. He was finally going to see Ara after all this time.

CHAPTER 24

Raina's phone buzzed with a call from her stepmother.

"Barry can't get in touch with Ara. Have you talked to her lately or is she off drunk in a ditch somewhere?"

Raina pulled on one of the doctor's T-shirts and flattened out her hair. "Not in a few days, we aren't exactly speaking. You know how she can be."

Arabelle sighed deeply into the receiver. "Who in her situation would refuse to talk to their lawyer? She is not even paying for it, dammit. Did she say anything to you that should make me feel alarmed?"

"I told you. She's not talking to me."

Distracted, Raina realized she had the opportunity to snoop around the doctor's apartment, to find out more about who he is. She opened a few drawers, but nothing alarming stood out to her. If she really met a good guy, then she guessed something good came from her horrible brunch with Ara. Her thoughts were interrupted by Arabelle's continued demands. "You need to get her to speak with her lawyer. Do you understand me? I'm sure I don't need to remind you of our agreement. Those checks I've been sending don't get signed for nothing."

Arabelle never missed an opportunity to remind her of the monthly checks she sent Raina to watch over Ara.

"Got it. You don't need to remind me, I understand. She's just so goddamn difficult these days."

"That's not really my problem, is it, dear? Years ago, you said you could handle her."

"And I can."

"She has a history, you know. Hasn't always been the sturdiest block in the building, if you catch my drift."

Raina had full knowledge of Ara's episodes of depression but usually chalked them up to an overload of wine and scrolling, resentfully, through others' Instagram feeds, not mental illness. Just a touch of envy to what others had that she wasn't able to accomplish. While many thought of Ara as a driven and hardworking young woman, always with her ducks in a row, Raina knew that was far from the truth. Ara could host the most pathetic pity parties for herself, but as dreary as these episodes were, Raina would never have classified them as unstable. She should, however, thank Arabelle. Her constant nagging and self-diagnoses of her daughter made it easy for Brad to convince Ara she needed help. They would have never been able to convince her to go to the facility had it not been for her mother constantly reminding her of her flaws.

"How unstable is she?"

"You just need to know there is a very dark side to her."

Raina mumbled, *I'll talk to her* before Arabelle hung up as quickly as she had called. Raina imagined what Ara would do if she found out her mother was spilling her secrets. In the beginning, when she first met her future stepmother, it was easy to see her relationship with her daughter was strained at best. Not every mother would speak so candidly to a near stranger about her daughter's issues, but that never stopped Arabelle. Raina knew the only reason Arabelle was present now was to manipulate the coverage and her make sure her daughter didn't ruin her reputation. She didn't trust her to handle the Bugias and their publicity powerhouses on her own.

Raina quickly dressed, wondering how to convince Ara to speak with Barry Goldberg without screaming the obvious. She scrolled through her contacts before stopping on Lane's number and quickly typed out a text message for him to call her ASAP. Within a minute, her phone was ringing. Raina cut right to the chase.

"We need to convince Ara to meet with her lawyer. I have a feeling she's avoiding him." Raina cut off Lane's protests with, "My mother told me. Can you help? It's for Ara, Lane." Taking a play from Arabelle's book, she hung up the phone before he could argue.

An hour later, Raina was sitting across from Detective Maro, warming her hands around a Styrofoam cup of burnt coffee. She had read once that precincts purposely keep interview rooms cold to make the subjects uncomfortable. Determined to play the part of a concerned stepsister, Raina had powdered her face and applied a neutral lipstick.

"What can I do for you today?" Detective Maro asked, tucking a few pages of notes behind the blank pages on his pad.

"There's something I think you should know regarding Brad's case," Raina started.

"You two were lovers, I know," Maro interrupted. "We subpoenaed his email and hard drive. We've learned a lot about you lately, Ms. Martin."

Her mind ran through all of the things that could be in those emails. All the details they could reveal about her affair with Brad that the detectives could share with Ara. "Yes, Brad and I were involved. In love, I could argue. But Ara, she has secrets, too. He wasn't the only one cheating, Detective."

"Isn't Ms. Hopkins your stepsister and friend?" Maro asked.

"She is," Raina replied. "Which is why I am here. I need to know that she did not do this to Brad as much as you do, and I want you to either prove that to me and the world, or lock her up and make her pay for what she did."

She could tell Maro was starting to get fed up with her family and the drama that came with them.

"Ms. Martin, I have to warn you that anything you say here can be used against you, or Ara, if it provides insight into a possible motive. Understand?"

160

"Yes," Raina replied. "I understand. I'm not here to throw my sister under the bus or to implicate myself in a murder. I receive enough attention when it comes to this case, and at this moment, I crave privacy more than the spotlight." While the statement may have lacked complete truth, Raina wanted their conversation to remain confidential. At least until the timing was right.

After all, she didn't even know if there was definitely another person in her sister's life, but there were only so many reasons to hide someone's identity in your phone. Raina continued with her interpretation of Ara's personal life, dropping hints at a possible affair with a man disguised as Danielle in her contacts, and if that was the case, there was the chance that the baby was not Brad's after all. Holding nothing back, Raina also filled in the detective about Ara's forty-eight-hour evaluation for severe depression and anxiety that she herself had a large part in persuading Brad to arrange.

Conveniently, she left out how it had been her idea to send Ara away in the first place so she could have time alone with Brad. Nor did she tell the detective that the professional conclusion from Ara's visit was simply exhaustion. Hopefully the details of the web she was spinning came together to form a motive. And the mental instability a perfect touch to back it up. Or at least enough for them to look closer at Ara.

Maro glanced back at the notes he'd jotted down before saying, "Ms. Martin, I have to ask since you're here. Did you have anything to do with the death of Brad Bugia?"

Unfazed by the question, Raina replied, "Absolutely not. I could never. Brad and I were two of a kind, you see. We loved each other very much."

"I believe you," Maro said. "But you have to realize you have as much of a motive here as Ms. Hopkins does. Maybe more. Maybe he told you about Ara's pregnancy and you lost it. Maybe he didn't want you anymore and you murdered him in cold blood because you couldn't have him leave you and return to your stepsister, who you obviously have minimal loyalty toward, if any. As detectives, we have to consider all the possibilities."

Raina stared back at the detective, careful not to shift her glance or feed into Maro's efforts to throw her off. Why would she be loyal to Ara? What did Ara ever do to deserve a loyal stepsister? Raina's life was just fine before it was uprooted to come save *poor Ara*. Arabelle and her father gave Raina everything that she wanted, and in return, she had them wrapped around her finger, until Ara's father passed away. That was when she became Ara's sidekick, always having to help her or do what was best for her stepsister.

"Brad Bugia was playing both his wife and you, Ms. Martin," Maro continued. "I'm sure you know you weren't his only side piece. Any one of you could have offed him. And don't forget the sad possibility that he did this to himself."

"Detective, you read the emails, did you not?" Raina said. "Brad was not tired of me. I don't think he would ever toss me away, like a *side piece.*"

The detective nodded. "Would you like to write an official statement?"

"You know the answer to that. I asked for this to be confidential, Detective. You can see how this could be sensitive information if it got out to the public or even just to my family."

The last thing Raina needed was Ara to find out about all of this and be out on the streets where she could confront her. Unless, of course, she already knew. Either way, she could not give her the opportunity to get back at her.

Maro returned with another pad and paper and slapped it down in front of her.

"If you change your mind. Please be as detailed as possible and try to keep it to the facts, the law requires more than speculation."

As she stood to leave, she could hear Detective Maro on the phone.

"What's your thoughts on the stepsister?" she overheard. "Well, she's here making a statement. Apparently, family means nothing in Jersey."

CHAPTER 25

Ara wanted to walk into Dan's office spewing confidence like a Victoria Secret model, but couldn't force herself to actually go through the doors of the building. They hadn't seen each other face to face in some time and had only spoken when he drunkenly texted her. And even those conversations became minimal over time as he had others to fill the gap she left. The older Ara got, and the more settled in life with Brad, she needed the doctor's attention less and less. Not that it didn't feel absolutely wonderful when one of his well-written messages surprised her. Seemingly popping up every time her mind had given up on him. She could hardly imagine what seeing him in person would do to her.

Yet, Ara tousled her hair into her best beach waves, Dan not being one for a pin straight hairdo, and found an old pair of Converse Chuck Taylors in her closet and walked all the way from the Grand Central subway stop to his office. Only Dan would prefer a girl in kicks over high heels. The Lexington line could have taken her closer, but she thought the walk up Park Avenue would do her good. But even the Park

Avenue charm couldn't extinguish the growing pit in her stomach. She had to face the man that her heart had a hard time shaking, and for what she could assume was a conversation about her husband's murder. *How romantic.*

The nerves wouldn't settle, and she found herself on a nearby park bench scuffing the mucky pavement with the soles of her sneakers.

Her phone vibrated, indicating a text message. Lane.

How's it going, the message read.

Ara quickly responded, maybe a little too quick for someone who's supposed to have her knees spread and feet locked in stirrups getting her lady parts investigated.

Fine, I should only be a little while longer. Ara was starting to become uncomfortable with how easy it was for her to lie, but she would do whatever she had to keep Lane from finding out about Dan.

I'm out front when done. Fire lane. Didn't want you to have to take the subway back.

A now all-too-familiar sense of panic came over her. If only she could go back to the days when her biggest worry was staying at work late and missing a pre-registered spin class that's cost wouldn't be refunded.

Not knowing how else to respond she said, *I'll be out in ten*. Ara couldn't remember telling Lane where the doctor's office was. Actually, she was confident that she hadn't, but who knew with her these days. Keeping track of the twists and turns to her everyday life was getting much more difficult. Was Lane picking up on her lies? Glancing diagonally across the street, she could see his undercover car sitting parked just over a block away in the fire line directly in front of the building she was supposed to be in. She could easily slip in the car and make it seem as if she had attended her appointment.

Hoping by some stroke of luck a gynecologist happened to rent space somewhere in the twenty-something story building shared with Dr. Dan, she gathered her things from the bench, straightened out her shirt and started down the street.

When she got to the car, the passenger door handle would not budge.

"You could have told me," Lane said, leaning up against the wall in the building entrance behind her.

"Told you what?" She had to play it cool, what could he know about her relationship with Dan?

"I'm a detective, babe, it's not hard for me to track someone down."

She supposed that did come with the territory. It was easier pulling the wool over Brad's eyes. Or maybe Brad just didn't care enough to learn her whereabouts.

"I am sorry, I," stumbling as tears began to build behind her Ray Bans, "I just didn't think you needed to know." She was going to have to tread lightly around Lane's reveal to find out just how much he actually knew.

"I'm really glad you're seeing someone. I've wanted you to see someone since it happened. You've been through hell. I don't know anyone who would be able to deal with this shit on their own and especially without the help of a professional."

Ara sat on the curb, her head falling into her open palms. This was all beginning to take a toll on her. Maybe she should be seeing someone for real. Unfortunately, her experience with Dr. Dan turned her off from seeking therapy. Lane sat next to her, slightly more scrunched in the space between the curb and car due to his six-foot-plus statue. He placed his right arm around her, pulling her in and kissing her on the top of her head. "I'm sorry, babe, I am so sorry this happened to you, and I'm so sorry I can't fix it for you."

Feeling like she had to tell at least a small portion of the truth to Lane she began, "I used to see Dr. Dan when I was younger. Teenage years. He helped me through some hard times after my mother left, and then my father passed away and, you know, he was there for me through all of that."

"I know, I am glad you had someone you felt connected with that you could go back to."

"I haven't actually been back; I'm trying to force myself to go."

Kissing her one more time, Lane said, "I could go in with you, if you want?"

That's the last thing she wanted, but again, she lied, "Not today, but I'd like that."

Comfortable in his arms, Ara tried to remember a time when Brad acted that selfless. She had loved that man with every ounce of her being but she couldn't tell anymore if he ever truly loved her back. And if that was the truth, that hurt more than any affair he could have had.

"Promise me you won't lie to me anymore," Lane pleaded as he helped Ara to her feet and unlocked the passenger side door.

"Promise." She kissed him before sliding into the seat, making a mental note that she would really have to thank him one day for worrying about her. Glancing up, she thought she saw Dr. Dan standing in the entrance. As Lane pulled out to take her home, she knew she'd have to figure out another way to have a visit with Dr. Dan.

CHAPTER 26

Back in his office, Dr. Dan slammed all the files from his desk.

If Ara hadn't ditched their meeting today, he may have had a better idea of where things stood with her, what she had shared with the police. Then he could better navigate their investigation of him. Even if they did know their past, could they possibly know he had been following her and Brad? He was more than cautious—not even Ara knew, or she would have demanded he stop. He needed to get Ara to meet with him, so he could tell her everything he knew about that night.

"What's going on in here?" Harley, his ever-loyal executive assistant, rushed in as quickly as her four-inch heels would allow, gathering the paperwork.

Dan sat with his back to his desk, nearly shaking with stress.

"Is this about the detective who's been calling all morning? Are you in trouble?" She sat next to him, pulling her pencil skirt down to cover her upper thighs. Dan traced his fingers up from her bent knees.

"No, but a patient could be. You know how I feel about my patients." Harley definitely knew—she had been a patient herself.

"Is there anything I can do to help you relax? You know I don't like to see you like this." Dr. Dan stood, facing her as she moved herself to her knees. Shaking his head, he picked her up in one smooth motion and placed her down on his desk.

"It's your turn," he said, pushing her skirt up, revealing a red lace thong. He pushed it to the side and began to return the favor from earlier this morning. Dr. Dan needed to do whatever it took to keep Harley in his corner right now. She could be extremely uneven; he didn't need her turning on him.

CHAPTER 27

Other daughters may have been thrilled with a surprise visit from their mother who lived across country, but not Ara. She knew her mother was trying to catch her off guard, without any time to prepare. She often said, "You can tell a lot about a person when they're on the fly."

Arabelle had knocked firmly three times on the door and then stepped to the side, out of view through the peephole. Lane answered, dressed only in a white V-neck T-shirt and a pair of boxers. When he woke Ara up with the news that her mother was at the door, she put on a floral negligée, knowing her mother would never approve.

"I can see you two lovebirds aren't even trying to hide it anymore." Arabelle slammed her purse down on the corner table. "Is anyone going to offer me a cup of damn coffee?"

Lane, exiting for the kitchen, said, "I'll put a pot on."

"What are you doing here?" Ara said.

"Happy to see you too, sweetheart." Sitting on opposite ends of the leather sofa, the tension between them was more than palpable.

"Jesus, Ara, act like you have some goddamn class."

"That didn't take long, Mom. Thanks for stopping by. The closest bar doesn't open until eleven, though I'm sure you have wine in your car. Shall I call the driver?"

"Relax, Ara, what do you want me to think with you acting like a whore? You rolling out of bed and greeting me in such a manner. It's beyond disgraceful, the dirt has barely settled over your husband's grave."

Trying not to let on that her mother's insults still stung, she chose a slightly higher road.

"Did Peter leave you, is that why you're here?"

"No, darling, believe it or not I was coming to check on you. Hoped we could get brunch, catch me up on things. You know, mother-daughter things."

"Lane and I were going to eat before my meeting today with Mr. Goldberg, which I'm sure you already know about." Mimicking Arabelle's tone, Ara said, "He's just catching me up on things."

"*Lane* does not have to take you. I'm here and he can go do whatever he does."

174

"It's his day off, and we spend it together. But since you're here, brunch it is." She stood and walked toward the back of the apartment. Lane appeared holding a single mug of coffee, presumably for Arabelle. Before he could ask questions, Ara said, "Let's shower, babe. My mom wants to take us to brunch." Looping her fingers through the belt buckles of his jeans, Ara leaned in and kissed him, selling the passion for her audience.

Arabelle cleared her throat non-apologetically, interrupting the scene. Lane handed her the coffee and said, "Make yourself comfortable."

Once back in the bathroom and alone, Lane's demeanor completely shifted, clearly unhappy with her stunt. "What the hell was that! Your mother now thinks I'm a pig."

"Who cares what Arabelle thinks? I've seen her twice a year since I was a teenager. You've slept over here more often than that." Ara was already undressed and in the shower.

"I care about us. And that probably means one day your mother is going to have to approve, don't you think?"

"No, I do not think that's what that means at all," Ara said. She opened the shower door and pulled him toward her. "This already works. Just let me have some fun with my mother. *Please*."

"I'm not just some manwhore, Ms. Hopkins. I have feelings, too."

"Didn't you hear my mother? *I'm* the whore." She splashed water on his face as he playfully pushed her back under the streaming warm water, joining her in the shower still wearing his boxer briefs. The water fell over their heads as he pulled her in, touching chest to chest.

"I love you, Ara." Not quite remembering what to say in return, she kissed him as the water washed over their faces.

"Don't make too much trouble with your mother today."

Ara pulled back from him dismissively. "You serious?"

"Just go see your lawyer, it could only help you."

Lane wrapped his arms around her waist from behind her as she grabbed the shampoo and massaged it into her scalp. "No need to cut off your nose to spite your face." Ara rolled her eyes and turned back to face him.

"Fine, but only because you asked."

An hour later, Ara and her mother worked through the general niceties more in line with a Monday morning conference call than a mother-daughter catch up date. Ara knew the call Lane had received to go into the station was bogus, but she didn't blame him. She wished to bail on this brunch herself. After determining the warmer weather was much needed, and that Manhattan's bustle never slowed, Arabelle finally came to the point.

"This will only make you look guilty, you know," she said, sipping her mimosa.

"Since when do you drink mimosas?" Ara wanted to tap dance on the table more than she wanted to entertain her mother's conspiracy theories.

"You can't hide from this, darling. Coping with losing your husband the way you are is downright cheap."

"My husband was murdered in cold blood while I dragged my pregnant self up the stairs, only to walk in on his life freshly taken." Ara continued, ignoring the lack of response, "Then I found out that the father of my unborn child had slept with anyone over a C-cup in

Manhattan and preferred to send me off for my *attacks* so he could parade *his* tastelessness around the entire city."

"And sleeping with his best friend makes you feel better?" Her mother's tone did nothing to hide the repugnance she had for her decision. "People will hate you for this."

"You think I killed my husband, don't you?" Ara twisted the champagne flute with just two fingers, feeling delightfully perverse.

"All I've wanted is for you to be careful. Handle this the right way, with some class."

Their shared order of poached eggs and an arugula salad was placed in the center, followed by a third round of drinks, despite both having lost their appetites.

"Anything else I can get you?" the waitress asked.

"Just the check, please." Ara couldn't last another ten minutes. "We have an appointment to keep."

Ara waited outside while her mother paid the bill and collected the to-go carriers the restaurant manager insisted on packing.

Arabelle had asked her driver to pick them up out front of the restaurant. "You should speak with Raina."

Flinching at her mother's statement, Ara said, "Why do you say that?"

"I can always tell when you two are arguing, does neither of you any good, you know."

How her mother could be so out of touch continued to amaze Ara. This was all Raina's fault. She was the one who unforgivably screwed Ara over, yet here her mother was asking her to make amends. If only she knew what Raina had done to her.

"We're not fighting. Just don't have anything to say to each other at the moment." Ara paused turning toward her mother. "She's not capable of understanding me and there are things that you don't know that happened between us. Things even you would agree are unforgiveable."

"You need support right now, people to lean on and to help you move forward. So what they don't know exactly how you feel."

Ara's eyes began to sting with unannounced tears. "I am being taken care of. Lane has been so kind and amazing. I don't know how I would be getting by without him."

Arabelle kicked at a stray cigarette on the sidewalk, grunting. "I see that now based on this morning. You certainly are being *taken care of*."

How could her mother think her relationship with Lane was nothing more than sex? "He's a good man. And Brad loved him like a brother. Brad would trust him to take care of me and you should, too."

"That may be so, but have you thought at all how it could be spun? Especially collecting on his insurance, shacking up in the apartment you shared with your husband."

"The insurance was your idea. I never wanted any of that."

Her mother may have a point, but she was certainly not going to admit to it. Her relationship with Lane was not something she wanted to advertise. Though she could assume the detectives may have picked up on it. "No one knows but you. And if you cared about me and my life moving forward, you would support me and not worry about Raina."

"I'm not going to tell anyone, darling. Just, please, spend a little less time locked away in your lingerie and more time proving to the world you are a good woman who was struck by a very tragic accident."

Ara didn't want to prove anything to anyone. She just wanted to close her eyes and wake up in someone else's world.

"Please call Raina, for me. It's always better when you two can support each other."

It was the last thing Ara wanted, but to silence the conversation with her mother she said, "Fine. I'll call her. Can we go in and get this meeting over with?"

CHAPTER 28

Though happy to get out of what was sure to be a sufficiently awkward brunch, Lane was not totally sure if the phone call he'd received would lead to a better afternoon. He didn't want to worry Ara by telling her he was called by the NJPD for standard questioning or that he was going to cooperate and go down to the station. Detective Ameno seemed to have the hots for him and Ara and stubbornly refused to respect the boundaries. Lane could bet the interview would be less than cordial. Especially after the last interaction between the two of them.

A seasoned detective himself, Lane could tell they thought there was more to the story. He didn't blame them one bit; he felt it, too. Sitting opposite Detectives Ameno and Maro, Lane felt uncomfortable with the tables turned. Ameno was standing, one foot up against the wall, perched up like a fierce flamingo, while Maro sat at the table, casually jotting things down he would want to remember later.

"You and Ms. Hopkins have grown closer, correct, Detective?" Maro asked, barely looking up from his yellow note pad.

Lane knew the tactic, start off with the small, more general questions, to make the person you're interviewing feel a sense of relief, only to ultimately throw them off guard. It was one he used often and was not going to fall for today, not with these clowns. "We were always somewhat close, Ara was married to my best friend. I was the best man at their wedding. Our friendship is nothing new."

"According to the maid of honor, Ms. Raina Martin, you had been keeping your distance as of late. Avoiding the circle of friends."

"I was working a lot of overtime. I'm sure you both can understand that."

Lane could never understand how Ara and Raina remained friends. He supposed they had to be cordial, being stepsisters and all, but he never understood the friendship side to their relationship, not with Raina's well-known meddling and attention-seeking ways. The two seemed like polar opposites to him. "You have to watch out for Raina. I'm sure by now you've learned she has a flare for dramatics." Clearing his throat, Lane moved his attention to Ameno. "Not to mention for . . . shall we call it, male attention?" He wouldn't put it past Raina to try seducing the younger detective, just to force her involvement in the case.

She hated being left out of a situation or ignored. It is was why he himself deliberately did not take notice of her when they all first met. Not that she hadn't made many desperate attempts to get with him, but he always preferred class to easy ass.

"Yes. We can see Ms. Martin likes to be, what *shall we* call it," said Ameno, returning the subtle jab, "involved. Are you getting a little *ménage trois* action there, Bene?"

Lane stood, his metal chair slamming as it fell back to the ground. "Don't you ever put those two in the same sentence to me." Knowing better than to further lose his composure, he stopped himself and reached for the fallen chair before his emotions got the best of him.

Ameno laughed and raised his hands above his head as if to mockingly prove his innocence. "That girl's really rocked your world there, huh, Bene? You help her kill her husband to continue your little tryst?" Lane had Ameno up against the wall before anyone knew what happened. Maro grabbed him, pushing Lane back toward the chair.

"Get your shit together, boys, you're both men of the law. I didn't think I had to goddamn babysit."

Ameno crouched low now, his face even with Lane's and unwilling to back down. "So whipped by Ara Hopkins. I bet you helped her kill her husband." A more mature detective would have backed off out of respect, but it was obvious that once Ameno got going it was hard for him to back off. "The headlines just got even better, you pathetic excuse for an officer," he said, sending Lane charging again.

Maro slammed his cell phone onto the table, bits of shattered, overpriced plastic pulverized the tension in the room, stopping both men in their tracks.

"Do I have to remind you two this is a high-profile murder investigation? Calm your egos and sit the hell down."

Ameno huffed and adjusted his jacket and then his tie and returned to his place against the wall. The animosity in the room was undeniable. Lane, again massaging his temples, cleared his throat. "Does he need to be in here?"

"He's a detective on this case."

"I'd prefer just to speak with you, assuming you're the lead. He can watch from the hall if he'd like but I refuse to be treated like a goddamn criminal. I've come here on my own terms and have no problem lawyering up with the precinct if necessary."

Maro turned his attention to Ameno and nodded his head to the door. Scoffing, Ameno kicked back at the wall, punching his fists. His glare never left Lane as he left the room, placing his own phone down on the table to record the conversation since Maro had busted his.

The remaining detectives sat quietly, Lane taking in a few shallow breaths.

"Detective Bene, may we begin?"

Lane nodded. "I've told you most of my history with Brad right up to the moments before he was killed. We were lifelong friends; our fathers were friends. I would have happily taken that bullet for him."

"Yes, you have been extremely cooperative but our questions today are more focused on your current relationship with Brad's widow, Ara Hopkins. You know we need to work all scenarios and consider any possible motive that presents itself."

"I am aware." Lane would cooperate for sure, but he was not going to give the detective more than he needed to. "Ara and I have grown closer since Brad's death, that's true. It could be because she's lonely, missing someone in her life. She's estranged from her mother and was close with her father, but he passed. With Raina as a stepsister, and your partner following her around town, it's my guess she's looking for someone she trusts to keep close to her."

"She's uncomfortable with the amount of questions from the department?"

Lane shifted in his seat. "Not just the department. The media, Congressman Bugia, her mother and friends. Everyone wants a piece of her these days."

"So you're shielding her from the questioning, keeping her company?"

"Something like that."

Maro shifted through his folder, pulling out what Lane could see was the official report from forensics.

"Your prints were found on the gun, Detective."

"I would imagine they would've been. I told you the first night, Brad and I bought the gun together, practiced at a shooting range down in Lakewood over last summer. Something I'm sure you also have verified by now."

Lane could tell Maro was mulling over his answer. "Mmm hmm. So, you taught your best friend how to use the weapon that ultimately killed him? Does that make you feel any sense of responsibility in his death?"

"Why would it? He wanted to learn how to protect himself. And Ara. He worked with a lot of high-profile clients in some mucky situations. Some of them even had friends that most people would not want to encounter on the street."

Just then, Ameno returned to the room, mumbling an apology before sitting back at the table. Lane was willing to accept the small victory before continuing, "He said he had clients that were angry and the opposing sides often viewed Brad as the enemy. Some even went as far to think that the financial wins he organized for his clients were the same as stealing from them. Not to mention his involvement with his father on the political side of his job. Some people viewed it as double dipping or unethical. Brad knew this, learned the hard way after a few encounters that it could make him a target, and wanted to protect himself."

Ameno asked, "Any specific parties make threats to Mr. Bugia?"

188

"Not that I know of, not that he would tell me. We were on somewhat opposite sides of the law. Our conversations mostly revolved around sports and craft beer."

"Couple of good 'ole boys, huh?" Ameno snorted.

"Like I said, we've known each other since childhood. We knew what we wanted to talk about and what we didn't when we got together."

"The friggin' New York Yankees?" Maro shot Ameno a warning look.

"Rangers, Giants, you name it," Lane replied sarcastically.

"Were you aware of the fact the Brad Bugia and Raina Martin were having a pretty intense affair?"

While it should not have been surprising, Lane nearly choked on his own saliva. What would someone with a wife like Ara ever see in that tramp? He knew the shock was sitting unmistakably on his face. "I was not, Ara would be devastated. I knew he was having an affair, or many for that matter, but I didn't know he was involved with Raina."

Ameno tossed the stack of smut-filled emails across the table. Lane spun the forms around and scanned quickly through the evidence hoping it would reveal some sort of mix up. Why would his friend go looking in the gutter and put his marriage on the line for a girl like Raina Martin? Nothing special or significant about her whatsoever, though he guessed that was true of all mistresses.

"You're saying Ms. Hopkins does not know."

Lane could feel his heart racing. "She hasn't said anything about it. I'm not entirely sure she could handle finding out news like this."

"Not handle it, like you think that maybe she could snap?"

"I didn't say that." Lane wished he could bring his best friend back from the dead just to kick the shit of him and send him back six feet under. "She is mourning, seems a little lost. Her entire world fell at her feet. I'm just saying it would hurt her deeply to lose another person close to her. It was no secret Brad was a bit of a playboy but with her family, I would imagine that is an entire different level of hurt."

Maro retrieved the emails, tapped the bottom of the sheets to even the pages and tucked them back into the file. "He wasn't exactly hiding it, Bene. Anyone with some decent wherewithal could have found out what we know."

Lane paused. "Ara is trusting. She wouldn't dig out stuff like this."

"Maybe so, Lane. Or maybe she has you fooled, too. Have you considered that?"

"I think you two are barking up the wrong tree. Raina's much harder than Ara. I'm confident she would do anything to benefit herself."

"That is true, but Ara has seen these same emails. We were even nice enough to give her a copy to bring home. She hasn't mentioned this to you?" Maro paused, narrowing his eyes onto Lane. "Maybe you don't know her as well as you think you do."

"I would never question Ara's innocence, if that's what you are saying."

Not wanting to consider what the detectives were implying, Lane ended the interview. He was not one hundred percent confident in his statements, despite his best attempt at passing it off that he was. The only thing he was confident about was that Ara wasn't being completely honest with him.

CHAPTER 29

Ara hoped Mr. Goldberg was prepared for the type of crazy he was about to encounter. From the beginning, she had tried to speak with him as little as possible. Something about talking to her lawyer made her feel guilty, so she happily allowed most of the arrangements to be made through her mother. Ara knew Arabelle Ridener and her deep wallet would persuade him to be involved in her new horror-show of a life.

"Ms. Hopkins, please sit," Barry said motioning toward an oversized leather chair across from him. His desk was tucked away in a comfortable corner office in midtown above Park Ave, which was bustling with the corporate afternoon foot traffic that came with the central location. Ara moved hesitantly toward the chair and extended her right hand to shake his.

"Ara. It's a pleasure." Ara loosely gripped his right hand, hoping they hadn't met in those first days. If they did, she didn't remember, making her fear she was far worse than she thought back then.

"You've been a difficult one to track down as of late, Ara," Barry said, leaning back in his chair.

"I apologize, but I'm sure you can imagine this has all been a lot for me to take in." Ara cleared her throat.

"My daughter has been through so much, Barry, the detectives are tailing her, they're approaching her on the streets when she's trying to move on with her life and enjoy a simple birthday brunch with my stepdaughter."

Ara's eyes shot to her mother as a silent warning sign to let her speak.

"Yes, I can imagine. These types of situations are not ones most people are prepared for," he said, pausing before continuing, "and many times normal life doesn't seem so normal after the fact."

"You can say that again," she said calmly.

"The problem is, I can't help you if you ignore my phone calls. It is common sense you see, if you refuse to talk to me, there's not much I can do. I see it a lot with clients, denial, people don't want to admit they have found themselves in a situation that requires legal representation, but the fact of the matter is, there could be charges, and those charges are serious, my dear. If I don't have a solid background on the case, it is only going to hurt us both in the long run."

The last thing Ara needed was another lecture. So what, she ignored a few voicemails.

Arabelle cut through her train of thought, "Well, Barry, that is one of the reasons why I hired you. You have a knack for being even-keeled even with the most difficult clients like my daughter. You are phenomenal at your job, and now she's here, so let's move past this. Ara is innocent, difficult," Ara scoffed before Arabelle continued, "but she is innocent and willing to work with you however necessary moving forward. So, let's get back to what we are paying you for."

"You pay me to defend her, to keep her out of jail, if necessary. You also pay me to protect her in the shit storm justice system that is swallowing her whole. Neither of which I can do if I have no contact. But I digress." He leaned forward and clasped his hands together. "So, Ara, let's start with the pregnancy. Based on communications I've had with their team, Congressman Bugia is pretty upset they weren't made aware of their coming grandchild. The comments have not been particularly kind to you, but not condemnatory either. I don't think it is helping your image by staying silent on this issue, especially when they are in the media vocalizing the need for a resolution to Brad's case."

Well, that would explain why they stopped talking to me, Ara thought, silently cursing her in-laws for further complicating her distressing situation.

"Are you saying she should go on the news, share her side?" Arabelle asked, again interrupting before Ara could get a word in.

"It could make her appear more sympathetic."

"I need to go on TV to appeal for *sympathy?*" This time Ara laughed out loud. "I find myself wishing more and more that I never even met Brad, if this was going to be our ending, what the hell was the point? I would have been better off never to have known him at all than to be thrown into this."

Barry tipped his head slightly. "Well my dear, unfortunately hindsight is 20/20, I suppose, and you could never have known this was going to happen. People only know what has been told to them and a lot of that has been what has come out after his murder. You can tell them what they don't know. What your life was like before."

Ara nodded, heeding the warning. "It's been a domino effect. I've learned a lot of things about him and lost faith in what I thought we had," she said, tucking each side of her loose hair behind her ears before continuing, "You can tell why I have been avoiding sharing my story to the media and the world."

"I am sure it doesn't help that people have a lot to say about your situation."

"No," Ara said, "it certainly doesn't. People are judgmental assholes."

Barry puffed an overemphasized exhale. "Well, you tell me what you want to do."

"I guess if the Bugias are out there villainizing me then I may need to change the tone, and I guess I would need your help with that. I feel I haven't been properly represented." Barry jerked to defend himself but Ara cut him off. "I don't mean by you, of course, properly represented in the media."

With Ara requesting privacy from the very beginning, the media had only been left with tidbits of information from secondary sources. While there was something to be said for hibernating during a time of grief, there was also great risk in allowing the public to form their own opinions of her. She now understood the media needed to see the tears soaking her face, her joining the desperate cries for justice. The public needed to feel involved with her pain—and, of course, deem it believable.

"Brad was no altar boy. I always knew that, but since his death I have learned incredibly sordid details of exactly who he was. He cheated, abandoned me during moments of need, put his personal interests and pleasures over our child-to-be, and forced me into many repulsive situations. He wasn't the type many would want to spend their life with, if you catch my drift."

Arabelle couldn't sit back any longer. "Those are all extremely difficult things to deal with, Ara, but I'm not sure smearing his family's good name is the best strategy here. It can make you come off as bitter, hostile even. Someone who could have been looking for revenge."

"I am bitter. I'm confined to tabloid hell because of him." She could feel her cheeks beginning to heat, and she tied her hair into a top knot high on her head as she took an exasperating breath. "But that's not what I want to show the world at all, and that's not what I'm suggesting."

Arabelle and Barry eyed her with piqued interest. "I am going to say that I knew everything. Was accepting of his flaws, happy to be moving forward with him as my partner and that he was committed to the same. I don't want people thinking that I was blindsided by all this, I want them to believe that I forgave him and that we decided to move past the cheating and the lying and live a happy life together."

Contemplating the strategy, Barry said, "It's a difficult thing to do, Ara. It's hard to appear genuine with a relentless reporter pouncing on you like a rabid animal. They come for blood and ratings."

"I was a good wife."

Exhaling he said, "Fine, I'll make some calls, see who wants the interview."

Ara turned to her mother. "Happy now?"

But her mother looked anything but happy with her. "Am I the only person here who thinks she won't do well on air by herself? Up until this morning, she's been hiding off in bed with Brad's best friend. They're going to eat her alive!"

Barry rolled his eyes, bringing both hands to his brow. "Of course she has been."

Ara hated how her mother always found a way to make her feel like the smallest person in the room. She should have known she wouldn't allow this meeting to end without publically shaming her for her sex life.

"Then we send someone on with her. Create a buffer, so to speak." Barry moved his attention to her. "And not your new boyfriend."

The three sat in strained silence, considering the options.

"What about your stepdaughter, Raina, she was on once before, wasn't she?"

Ara peered down her nose at Barry. Raina didn't help her the first time. Then again, did she need her to help her this time? What if there was a way she could use Raina to her benefit. Discreetly expose her for all the world to see? It wouldn't be easy, but she could do it. Raina doesn't know that she knows about her affair with Brad and exposing her on television would be like a sucker punch to the gut.

"I think that would be a great idea," Ara said, cutting into the conversation.

"I thought you two weren't speaking?"

Feeling suddenly optimistic, Ara smiled at her mother. "You wanted us to make up, didn't you? I'll talk to her and apologize for ruining her birthday brunch. I think I'll feel more comfortable with family there."

Arabelle, delighted by the decision, returned the smile. "OK then, that's settled. Barry, you can make the arrangements?"

"Certainly. I'll make some calls, see who wants the interview."

Ara stood, extending her hand as if she'd just made a gentleman's deal with the devil. With a firm shake to Barry, she smiled knowing he had no idea what she was planning.

"I will text you when I hear back," Barry said, shaking her hand. "If you are OK with that form of contact, of course. Phone calls don't seem to be your thing."

"That works for me."

Now all she had to do was stomach up an apology to Raina.

CHAPTER 30

Raina wasn't expecting anyone at her apartment so when Ara knocked, she couldn't think who it could be. What should have been relief to see a familiar face standing on the other side of the door instead created a volatile wrenching in her stomach. She was beginning to understand what it meant when people referred to others as 'unraveling.' At first she'd been surprised at how easy it was to keep up with the lies she'd been spinning over the past few years, but recently her instincts were starting to go wrong.

To Raina's dismay, Ara looked beautiful as always, even with the recent stress. Despite looking slightly more put together than previous months, Raina could tell she was nervous by the way she was fumbling with her phone, attempting to look preoccupied. Ara always used her phone as a protective armor when she was left alone. Poor thing was too insecure to sit alone for five minutes. Raina often tried to show up for their planned meetings first, for that reason. Unless she was angry with her. Then she would let her sit and wait in her own discomfort.

"Come in." The two ended up in the living area on the same couch Ara had spent so many weeks after Brad's death. She settled in her favorite corner with Raina adjacent to her, both curling their feet up underneath them.

"I wanted to come by and say I'm sorry about brunch the other day. I know you love your birthday, and I shouldn't have caused an issue like that." Raina knew she wasn't an easy person to apologize to, usually expecting people to flat out embarrass themselves before she accepted. "Everything's been so messed up, and I really need you right now. I'm not expecting you to understand, I hardly understand myself anymore. I just wanted you to know that I didn't mean what I said."

"We barely even seem like we're friends let alone sisters these days. Friends call each other, see each other, at least pretend they are interested in each other's lives. I only hear from you if you need me for something."

Ara shifted her position on the couch. "I know, and it's my fault. I'm closing people off. I don't know why exactly, everything changed for me when Brad died. It ripped my guts out and, honestly, I don't know how the hell to deal with it." For a second, Raina thought Ara might cry, but her stepsister put her big girl pants on, it seemed. "But that's not your fault, and I need to start working through this shit on my own, not drag down everyone with me."

Arabelle must've spoke to her, Raina thought.

Surprisingly, the thought of Ara caving to Arabelle's demands lifted Raina's face into a smile. When she first saw Ara, she was sure she'd make her grovel, but watching her take the blame was enough. "I have been a good sister to you."

"Yes, you have been."

"There is no handbook for this. You're not the only one to blame for our fight. I've thought a lot about it recently, and maybe I haven't been doing everything I could to help you through this. It's just uncharted territory for me."

"You're not a doctor, nor should it be your problem to help me move on from something as traumatic as this."

"True. I guess all I can do is distract you from everything."

Despite barely making C's in college, Raina was a gifted debater and could probably persuade a person to jump off a bridge while convincing them it was their idea to do so. Without a doubt, Raina would not end this conversation with her step-sister until the blame was on Ara and her alone.

"And that's exactly what you have been trying to do, Raina. I am sorry."

Raina stood and walked to the small kitchen in the rear right corner of the apartment. "Want anything?"

"Sure, whatever you're having." She returned moments later and handed Ara a large glass of tomato juice mixed with vodka. Both girls took large sips before placing the glasses down on the table.

"I met someone, you know. Think it could be going somewhere," Raina confided, interested to see Ara's reaction.

"Wow, that's really awesome. They always say spring is the perfect time for a new relationship."

"He's a *doctor*."

Ara laughed a little and pushed her nose up mockingly. "Well, look at you!" Both girls relaxed slightly, laughing at the prospect of Raina becoming an Upper East Side doctor's arm candy.

"You'll have to meet him if things ever get to that point. I don't want to push it, but he's practically perfect. I'm still in the grace period to determine if he's a psychopath, but so far so good. You know, taking it slow. There has to be some reason he's still on the market."

"I'm sure he was just focused on his career. How did you meet him?"

"Actually it was after our brunch. I tripped while walking. He helped me up while others just stood there laughing at me. Kind of romantic, actually, we spent the rest of the night at his place. Getting to know each other."

"How very *Sex and The City*." Ara threw a nearby pillow Raina's way. "Well, Samantha Jones, hopefully you landed yourself an Upper East Side Prince Charming."

"One could only hope!"

After a brief pause, Ara jumped up, talking over her shoulder as she walked back to the bathroom. "I'm happy for you, girl."

Soon after Ara closed the bathroom door, her phone buzzed, flashing the caller *Lady Dr*.

Picking up the phone, Raina entered Ara's password and took a brief peek through the call list before opening the contacts. Danielle was noticeably no longer listed. Quickly clicking out of the contacts and back to recent calls, she selected missed and then Lady Dr. Maybe she was overthinking things, but she didn't remember this listed in Ara's phone the last time she snuck a look. They shared a gynecologist and Dr. Merrick was saved as precisely just that.

She dialed the number and a male voice answered almost immediately, obviously in some sort of distress.

"I am so happy you finally called."

"Yes," Raina said just above a whisper. "I don't have much time but I wanted to return your call." She did not want to give the caller too much information and decided it best to be vague, hoping this person would play along.

The other end went silent for a moment or two before the man answered with a hint of suspicion in his tone. "Ara?"

"Yes, this is she."

"I have to jump off the line. Please call the office to reschedule your appointment." The line went dead at less than one minute of clocked call time. Feeling more doubtful than ever, Raina was interrupted by the sound of the bathroom door opening. Quickly, she replaced the phone on the coffee table.

Ara returned moments later without seeming to notice the snooping that had taken place.

"Let's get out for a little bit." Raina stood, "How about a walk?"

Ara nodded as the two walked out of the apartment. Satisfied, Raina felt she got everything she needed from Ara's apology for today.

CHAPTER 31

Dr. Dan nervously patrolled his office as Harley consoled him to no avail.

"She knows what she is doing to me!" he yelled, tossing a few meaningless items from his desk. Harley, seeming startled by his anger, scurried about trying desperately to return the office to normal. He never acted like this in front of her, normally fearful it would rock her own fragile mental stability.

"Is there anything I can do for you? Anything at all?"

"Yes, Harley," he spit. "You can stop trying to crawl up my ass and make yourself useful in my reception area as I hired you to do!" He could tell his rage was penetrating her pores with its ugliness as she fought back tears, turned, and headed to the door.

Dan called after her, "Hold it together, Harley, I don't need you being an emotional wreck in front of my patients."

She slammed the door behind her. Dr. Dan knew as angry as she was with him, she would forgive him quickly enough. By late afternoon, in the lapse of his scheduled appointments, she would be bent over his desk, skirt up as he took her from behind.

She thrived off of his attention and would do anything for him. Harley loved him. He was aware that like many before, she hoped he was falling in love with her, too. Ultimately, he would disappoint her like he had the others. After his twisted relationship with Ara, he was never able to fully commit to anyone. It was impossible to build an emotional connection with someone in the present without letting go of the past. Over the years, he preferred watching Ara from afar to going through the motions with someone else. His obsession grew gradually, at first he'd dial her number after too many cocktails, just to hear her voice. But when that wasn't enough he had to find another way to get his fix. Occasionally he was ashamed of his behavior, fearful that someone might catch on to him. But neither Brad nor Ara ever noticed, and he was able to follow along with her in life. Watching her move on effortlessly stung. Did she ever love him?

With Brad out of the picture, he could finally see her again. If only she knew what he had for her, she would have shown up to their meeting. He had to convince her. If he could do that, he could get what he wanted. To see her, in person, alone, just him and her. Make her see that she could want him again. He knew he could convince her if given the chance.

CHAPTER 32

"Why do I have to go?" It was the first time Lane saw a childish side to Ara's normally polished composure.

"Because that is what people do in situations like this. They talk to someone, work through shit. It's pretty standard, Ar, something horrific happens, you see a shrink to help you deal with it."

Ara coiled her hair into a loose knot on the top of her head. Her tank top, which was anything but form-fitting, hung from her frame, revealing the slightest dip at the side of her breasts. Lane loved her like this, casual and dressed down. To him, it was when she looked the most beautiful. Ever since she met with her lawyer, it was like a weight had been lifted from her and she was finally able to exist more freely. Whatever the lawyer told her, it must have been good. Lane was over the conversations about Brad and his double-crossing ways.

"You look so beautiful right now, the last thing I want to do is talk about this damn case." Bothered, Lane moved between her legs as she sat on the side of his bed and leaned down, touching his forehead to hers. He remained there, forehead to forehead for a few moments, before planting his lips in her hair. "I can't help you get past this if you don't let me, baby."

Ara fell back onto the bed and rolled on one side, pulling the comforter over her bare legs.

"It makes it real, Lane. I've never wanted this to be real, can't you understand that? If I talk to someone, really talk to someone, it brings everything back, and then I have to relive it over and over again. Don't you understand I just want to forget it, try to move on without rehashing it every damn day."

Lane placed a hand to her lower back. "But it is real, babe. As real as it gets. You have to be in the best place mentally to deal with all of this. Both of our prints are on that gun. You know what that looks like for the police? We have to stay ahead of them and we can't do that if you aren't healthy."

Ara shot up, forcing Lane to jump back in reaction to her sudden movement. "When did you speak to the police about me?"

"They called me in. I had to. Obviously, you forgot I'm a detective myself. Jesus, Ara, calm down!" Once again, they met face to face but this time with burning conviction.

212

"When were you going to tell me this?" she demanded, sweat forming at her brow, something he noticed happened when she was stressed. "I trusted you."

"I think the real question is why the hell you're this upset. You look like you're gonna throw up. This is what I'm talking about, you can't overreact like this over small things like me meeting with the police."

"It may seem small to you, but I just don't like people talking about me! And everyone around me seems to be talking, and I'm sick of it!" Ara darted to the front door, grabbing her cell phone from the bedside table on her way. "I already had one lying husband, I don't need someone else in my life like that. Stay the hell away from me for now." Lane opened his mouth to argue, but she was already out the door and clearly not interested in his apology.

***

Dr. Dan was thrilled to get Ara's call. Of course he didn't mind meeting her at his apartment; he would meet her anywhere. Plus she sounded stressed and was short-winded on the phone. So he picked up the essentials from his desk—phone, keys, and wallet—and locked his office door behind him. Maybe he was acting paranoid, but Harley seemed to be extremely interested in where he went these days, and after his outburst, the last thing he needed was her snooping around.

"I'm taking an early lunch," he said, offering no further explanation.

But now he paced the apartment, his head flooded with possible scenarios. Already twenty minutes late, maybe, like last time, she wouldn't show at all. All he could do was wait. Nervously he picked at minor details in his living room until a text flashed across his phone's screen.

Downstairs.

He raced to the call button to notify the doorman. Moments later, Ara was standing in front of him, modestly dressed and stunning as ever.

Dr. Dan slowly crossed the room and reached out to her. She accepted his embrace and held onto him for a short while before backing out of his arms. "It's been a while, Doctor."

"Yes, too long, Ara. I've missed you." He nervously fumbled with his hands before patting the cushion on his couch. "Sit, please. God, I can't believe you're here."

Ara walked over to the sofa and sat next to him, retreating when he put a hand on her leg. Picking up on her signals, Dr. Dan quickly moved his hand back to his own lap. "How are you doing?"

"Better than you would think."

"I'm so glad. You look wonderful."

Sitting in an uncomfortable silence, they each kept their distance, feeling the other out for the first move. Ara's phone buzzed, and she read quickly through a text message, then tucked her phone into her purse. "You said you had something I needed to know about the night Brad was killed. So here I am."

"Well, first and foremost, I wanted to check up on you. I care for you, Ara, and obviously, you are going through some shit."

"It's been years, though."

"Yes." He swallowed, considering his next words wisely. "Doesn't mean I haven't thought of you. Not a day goes by where I don't think of you fondly. I still love and care for you a great deal."

Her eyes held his, unmoved by the endearing phrase. "Don't talk like that. Love is a very weighted word."

Dan wanted to pull her into him, tell her everything was going to be all right. Comfort her like he used to when the world stomped her down. He could see through her attempts at holding her shell together, and more than anything he wanted to let her fall apart. "I know you, Ara, and I know this must be very difficult for you."

And he did know her. Dan may not have seen Ara since she'd left him feeling used and tossed away years earlier, but he'd had access to her innermost thoughts since she was a teenager. No man could ever compete with that—not even Brad. In Dan's office, she'd revealed who she truly was: an abstract painting of competing emotions—adventurous and reserved, a touch psychotic but with a worldly intelligence. Ara Hopkins was a little bit of everything, and depending on the day, her character could reveal many traits. There was a time when he thought she was truly capable of anything. Maybe even murder, and that honestly turned him on.

"You knew a teenager, *Doctor*. Not the woman I am today. Our relationship was wrong on so many levels. It took me a long time to realize that you don't know anything about me anymore."

He tried not to look visibly hurt as he sank into the couch, holding his head in his hands before looking back up at her, his eyes begging for some indication that she still cared for him. "You've always been the brightest light in my very, very dark world. It may not have been right, but I've never regretted a moment of what I did with you."

She raised her hand, slapping him hard across his right cheek before crumpling into a pile of free-flowing tears. "I don't know why I came here," she sobbed. "I promised myself I would never need you again. You were never any good for me."

He brushed the loose hairs from her eyes. It killed him to see her flinch to his touch. "I've always needed you, Ara, don't you get that?" He moved in to comfort her, placing his hands on her shoulders.

"No, you've always needed me behind closed doors! Even when I was old enough, I was never good enough for you in public. It always had to be in secret. Do you know what that felt like? Feeling everyday like I wasn't good enough for you?"

"Please forgive me. For everything, Ara." He took another move closer to her, almost unable to hold himself back from scooping her up in both arms.

"This was a huge mistake," she said as she tried to brush him away to stand and leave, but he grabbed her arms, holding her close to him. Ara threw her weight against him, but he wouldn't let go of her. She tried to slap him, but he held tight to her wrist as she kicked her legs, feverishly trying to break from his hold. He pulled her down and onto her back and tightly secured her wrists above her head.

"Shhhhh, baby, I'm not going to hurt you. You need to calm down." His forearms were now pressed to her body holding her to the floor. Her face was soaked with tears. "Be a good girl, Ara. I'm not going to hurt you." It was more difficult than he anticipated, to be this close to her. His mind raced back to all of the times he had made love to her, back when she welcomed him on top of her. Losing control, he kissed her lips, then her neck and chest, forcing himself onto her as she squirmed and fought against him underneath.

When she tried to yell, he quickly put his right hand over her mouth, his left still holding her wrists. She bit down hard on his hand.

"What the hell, Ara!" Dan yelled, not expecting that escalation. He jumped back, releasing her wrists. She rolled over to her stomach and got to her feet, barely taking a step toward the door before he yelled, "I know who killed your husband!"

Ara stopped dead in her tracks, then crumpled to the floor. She was out cold. He leaned over and gathered her into his arms, holding he against him, delivering a single kiss to her cheek.

After moving her to his bed, he laid with one arm draped loosely over Ara's waist, finally feeling what he had hoped for when she walked in the door. He knew there would be something raw between them, but hoped when she saw him the warmth would come back to push out the bad. He leaned in closer, kissing the bare skin at the base of her neck. With his eyes closed, he took it all in. For two years now he'd wanted to be back in this position and had used many unknowing women as space holders, desperately searching for the one who could distract him. But his infatuation for Ara Hopkins ran deep, and as he'd learned, it was insatiable. No other woman could ever quench his thirst.

CHAPTER 33

Desperate to find Ara, Lane paced her apartment, thinking of who she would run to or if she would run to anyone at all. Thank God he'd traced the mystery friend *Danielle's* number he had seen in Ara's phone weeks ago. His gut feeling that the tone was off in the messages had been spot on. Danielle was in fact Dr. Daniel DaVedere, an unconventional therapist on the Upper East Side who had a practice in the building he picked her up at a week ago. He wasn't pleased that Ara felt she had to lie to him about seeing a therapist, but he wasn't angry either. With everything his poor girl had been through in the past months, living in such a public turmoil, he felt she deserved a few secrets. Especially if they were as harmless as seeing a shrink.

He typed the doctor's name into the search bar on his phone and clicked the call option. A bubbly, young receptionist answered.

"I'd like to speak with Doctor DaVedere, it's important," Lane said, hoping it was common practice to hold back on the details.

"Dr. Dan is out for lunch at the moment. Can I take a message?" Lane may have been digging, but he thought he noticed a slight tremor in the receptionist's voice.

"Do you know when he will be back?"

"Unfortunately, he was called into an emergency situation. If you leave your name, I can have him return your call when he is back in the office." Under the woman's well-practiced receptionist voice, Lane sensed something amiss.

"I'll call back tomorrow, thanks." He hung up the phone and grabbed his keys. He hoped he'd be able to get more out of Dr. Dan's receptionist in person than over the phone.

CHAPTER 34

Ara woke on her back, pillows propping her head and knees, a cold washcloth covering her eyes, and a familiar body next to her breathing ever so slightly. For a minute or so she kept still, recalling the security Dr. Dan had once provided. Unfortunately, he now offered nothing she wished to indulge in. At one point of her life she wanted nothing more than to feel the full extent of his love, but here, laying in his bed as a grown woman, she wanted to blame him for everything he truly was. The first man in her life to be full of words whose actions never reciprocated. Who professed feelings disguised as passion and a man who robbed her of her youth by allowing her to grow up too quickly. Her buzzing cell phone transported her back to reality. *Lane*.

"I need to get that."

"I'll grab it for you," Dan said, swinging his legs to stand on the opposite side. "Seems like your friend Lane really needs to reach you. Your phone has been going off non-stop."

"I walked out on him, he's just worried," she said, slowly bringing herself to sit up, her head spinning.

"Seems a little controlling to me." Dr. Dan handed her the phone and she scrolled through the messages and missed calls. Seconds later, there was pounding on the door.

Wiping her face down with the wet washcloth, Ara exhaled, giving herself a moment before dealing with the escalating situation."

"Where is she?" she heard Lane insist as he forced himself inside when Dan opened the door. Knowing that Lane was losing his temper, she rushed to the bedroom doorway. Dan and Lane were face-to-face, flirting with making it physical.

"Lane! Stop it," she yelled.

"Are you kidding me right now?" Lane backed up, jolted to see Ara emerging from the doctor's bedroom.

"It's not what you think," Ara explained rushing over to him. "Please, Lane, don't be upset with me." Dr. Dan's eyes dropped as she rushed past him to comfort Lane. Standing on the tips of her toes, she brushed his hair back and kissed him, holding his two-day stubble in her hands.

"You're seeing your therapist in his bedroom now?" Lane demanded, looking crushed.

"I'm sorry I ran out, I really am, I'm so sorry." Ara kissed Lane again, releasing some of the anger from his body. Tears stung her eyes before becoming too much to hold in, staining her cheeks. Despite being angry at him for his lies earlier in the day, she realized she cared much more about hurting him than she'd thought she would. If he ever told her he loved her again, she knew she now had a response.

Lane drew her in, his left arm around her waist, his right holding the back of her head. Surrendering, he said, "Me, too, Ara. I'm so sorry I didn't tell you right away when they called." Quietly, she allowed a few more tears to fall on his shoulder. "You know I only want what's best for you. I just can't figure out what the hell that is right now, but I'm trying, I really am, Ara."

Dan cleared his throat before saying, "We can continue our conversation another time." Lane shot him a threatening glance. "At the office, of course."

Ara held tight to his hand, thankful he was willing to forgive her, remembering how stubborn Brad could be. "We can all talk. Right here, right now. You said you knew who killed Brad," she said with a challenging stare toward Dan. "Anything you were going to tell me about that night, you can do so in front of Lane."

She walked Lane over to the couch, sitting with her hand still in his. She wanted him to know that no matter what was said, she needed him. Dr. Dan hesitantly followed and sat on the edge of a single adjacent Victorian-style armchair.

"As I said, I called you here first and foremost to check up on you, Ara. Being a past patient and all," Dr. Dan began as Lane placed his hand on Ara's thigh. Dr. Dan continued, "Secondly, because I have reason to believe I know who murdered your husband, Brad." Ara felt Lane flinch at the mention of Brad from Dan's lips.

Lane jumped in before Ara could speak, "And what reason would you have to say something like this?" Ara was happy he did, remembering why she had passed out in the first place. What did Dan think he knew? Every scenario she could come up with was damaging.

"Forget it. I shouldn't have said anything."

Clearly angry and unsatisfied with the response, Lane stood. "You drag Ara over here with false promises, just to back out and pull this?!"

The two men began yelling and pushing each other, caught up in their own argument. Lane was the first to notice Ara had covered her ears and was rocking back and forth with tears pouring down her face.

"Stay the hell away from her!" Lane yelled to Dr. Dan as he lifted Ara from the couch and lead her toward the door.

"Ara, don't you want to know?" Dan called out, but Ara buried herself further into Lane's shoulder. *Did* she want to know?

Brushing the outline of her face, Lane kissed her. "The man's a freaking lunatic, you understand me?" he said as he set her down outside the apartment. "He doesn't know anything, he's just trying to get involved, who knows why. I don't think you should ever speak to him again. I'm sorry, but never."

Ara paused slightly and adjusted her tank top to better cover her chest, feeling exposed. "He tried to rape me, Lane. I didn't want to tell you . . ." But she couldn't finish, the damage had been done. Lane looked down at her, his eyes swelling with agony before he turned back to the apartment. Bursting through the door and grabbing Dr. Dan by the shirt, Lane lifted him from the ground before delivering a final blow.

CHAPTER 35

Ara gave Lane just enough information to keep him from prying further. They were now safely lying on her sofa, her head in his lap as he raked through her hair with his fingers. The TV hummed Netflix favorites in the background, filling the silence she knew he wanted to break so badly. She didn't blame him for having more questions. She had not been honest, to say the least, about her relationship with the doctor. Lane deserved so much better than that. And then to drop the rape bomb on him. The last thing she wanted to do was bring him down with her as her life spiraled out of control.

"He brought everything I did to him on himself. I need to know that you know that," Lane said, dancing his fingertips across her scalp. "I don't want you to think I'm a monster who has no control over his actions. I'm not going to let anyone do that to you ever. I would kill him first, you understand me? No matter the cost."

It was exactly what she was afraid of, Lane throwing away his life and his career for her.

"I could never think that. *He* is the monster, Lane. Not you. He could only hope to be as good of a man as you are." Ara rolled over onto her back to look up at him. His tortured expression focused ahead, looking through the television.

"I hate that after having a professional relationship with you for all of those years, he would even think to take advantage of you like that. And worse, at a time in your life when you need people to hold onto that you could trust. He's a coward, Ara. A no-good coward. You need to let me call it in. This is not going unpunished. He needs to pay."

If only he knew everything.

Ara sat up, gathering her hair over one shoulder. "Absolutely not. I'm not strong enough right now. Not to mention you have your own career to worry about and you are not jeopardizing everything you built for yourself over me." Knowing he needed more convincing she added, "You said it yourself. You can't protect me if your reputation is not intact at work. You need to remain detached from me, at least in the eyes of the law and your job. Dan isn't going to say anything, and we don't need to either."

228

"I didn't say anything about my reputation. I don't give a damn about that. Everyone knows I'm a good cop."

Ara looked at him, her eyes pleading. "You know what I mean, Lane. If Maro and that asshole Ameno trust you, and everyone else on the force does, too, you can protect me. You can protect us. You said so yourself that both of our prints are on that gun, we know we didn't do it and eventually everyone else will, too. Have you thought about *us* after this crazy nightmare is over? You told me you loved me, and we deserve one day to see if that's true. Maybe we can actually have a life together without all of this."

He sat back on the sofa considering all that she was saying. She knew she was winning him over.

"I need you to protect me, Lane. More than I need you to call in a lousy attempt at a sexual assault. I should have never gone over there, but that's on me, not you. It won't look good for you or me if you call this in."

Ara straddled him in a way that more resembled a bear hug than a sexual advance. She rested her chin on his shoulder and pulled him into her. "I need you, Lane. Right now, I feel like I can't lose you."

Lane pulled her in even tighter, kissing her cheek. "He'll get his. I'll make sure of it."

Ara closed her eyes, breathing in a successful attempt at getting her way, "Yes. I'm sure he will. You know what they say about karma."

After a long silence, Lane said, "Please don't run out on me again. Something worse could have happened. I don't want you to feel you have to prove anything to me like you had to with Brad. You don't need to run." The guilt in his voice was apparent, biting Ara with her own. Did she ruin every good man in her life?

Sitting up, she looked Lane in the eye, tracing his brow with each hand before kissing him. She pulled him in once again. "None of this is your fault, and you've been so good to me. I don't deserve a man like you, Lane Bene."

CHAPTER 36

As a therapist, Dr. Dan had learned early in his career that it was much easier to work on someone's past than hold high, unreachable hopes for the future. It was this notion that allowed him to see through Lane Bene, even back two years earlier, when he'd watched the happy wedding party from across the waterfront restaurant Ara had chosen for the rehearsal dinner. Not an invited guest, Dan had sat near the corner of the bar in an adjoining room, catching a glimpse at Ara every now and then as the happy couple mingled with the attendees, oblivious to his presence. Dan had wanted to break Ara free from Brad's half-assed hold for some time now. He saw how Brad's loose eyes were always drifting toward other women.

The way Lane looked at Ara directly contrasted with how Brad had. At first, Dan had assumed the best man may have had a few too many cocktails. It was only when the bride got to Lane's table that it became evident that, like himself, Lane Bene was drunk on Ara, not the open bar. The poor sucker could barely make eye contact and kept a catholic school inch between the two when she went in for a hug. The real tell was the way Lane watched her as she worked her way around the room.

Lane's hunger was not as primitive as Brad's lust for the maid of honor, though. Those two were practically licking their lips across the table from each other, ready to pounce when no one was looking, stirring the sexual tension to a steaming, palpable pulp. Brad and Raina had been playing their own game now for quite some time, toying with getting caught by Ara. Or anybody for that matter.

Dan always knew Brad was going to get his. The way he flaunted his arrogance and untouchable swagger. He once told Ara, "Even a king is bound to board," knowing his life would eventually catch up to him. For years, Dan had been certain there would come a time when the rosy façade would fade from Ara's world and she would see Brad for exactly what he was. A self-serving man who disguised himself in confidence and charm. Dan tried to keep close, so when her world came crashing down, he could step in and be there for her. From his years sitting across from Ara in his office, he knew she would need someone to pick up the pieces for her, fill the void she desperately needed full since her father's death. Sitting on the sidelines was not easy and patience was not a virtue he held. Yet for his Ara, he would have waited forever.

What he had not seen coming was Lane moving in on his queen.

Down at the station, he anxiously tapped his fingers together, one at a time, as he waited for the detectives. The bleak gray paint of the interview room and blasting air conditioning were meant to make people feel uneasy, nervous even, but he welcomed the simplicity of it and the cool air. It was easy for him to remain calm under pressure, even if his life was demanding as of late, even a bit overwhelming. Plus, he was there on his own accord. There was no reason for him to feel uncomfortable. Perhaps he would feel differently if he'd been dragged in off the street for questioning.

"Dr. DaVadere?"

Dan stood and shook each detective's hand and unbuttoned his suit jacket before sitting back down again in his chair. "Thank you for putting aside the time to meet with me."

"Of course, Doctor, what can we do you for?" Detective Ameno stood off to the side, back up against the wall.

"As you know, Ara Hopkins was a long-time patient of mine. She was one of my first, actually, right out of school and my continued education. Given our years of sessions, sometimes a few a week, I got to know her quite well. Those in her inner circle, too. Through her account, of course."

Ameno stepped forward, placing both hands on the table. "Yes, *her* version of those in her inner circle, and from what we could tell, you haven't treated her in a few years."

"Yes. That is what I said. Obviously, all of what I have heard has been through Ara's perspective, and it has been a while since we last met, however, in my experience you learn quickly to sift through and find out the reality within all these details."

The humming of the overworked air conditioner broke up what could have been an awkward period of silence. Maro looked over to Ameno before saying, "Understood. Still confused on why you wanted to have a sit down here, Doc."

"I am concerned with Lane Bene's involvement with Ara. I would predict she is quite vulnerable right now and he seems very, what you would call it—"

"Involved," interrupted Ameno.

"Yes. I know they were not particularly close before Brad's death. When I last saw her, she even spoke of how she was afraid that Brad's family and friends didn't accept her. I am concerned that he has manipulated her into some sort of relationship she is not capable of handling right now, with the trauma and all."

Maro, who seemed busy taking notes, finished jotting something down and said, "Got to be honest here, Dan. Not sure, one, how this is your concern, and two, why you thought to drag us all together to discuss who you think Ara Hopkins should be getting it from."

"It is exactly who she is 'getting it from' that I think should be vital to your investigation. There were times in the past where Ara confided how Lane made her uncomfortable and was standoffish toward her. Clearly now that is not the case. The two are practically inseparable!" He knew he had slipped up the moment the word *inseparable* left from his mouth.

Maro caught it, too, and wasn't about to let it slide. "And if you don't mind me asking, Doctor, how do you know about how much time they're spending together? You sure know a lot about Detective Bene and Ara for someone who hasn't even seen her professionally in years, according to your last statement. Is there another reason we should know why you feel personally involved in Ara Hopkin's life?"

Dan stood, but made sure to maintain eye contact. "I'm not sure what you are suggesting, Detective. I met with Ara earlier in the week to check up on her. I thought the facts I heard about Mr. Bene were concerning enough to come in. Clearly, I was mistaken." Dan re-buttoned his jacket and made his way toward the door.

"It's Detective Bene," Maro said. Dan noticed him staring at his jawline and bruised lip. "Get in a fist fight there, Doc?"

"Excuse me?"

"Your face. Looks like you took a right hook to the jaw."

Dan stiffened. His fists clenching, he turned and exited without answering.

CHAPTER 37

The detectives followed Dr. Dan out to the hall, knowing that as soon as the doctor turned the corner, he would practically smack right into Ara Hopkins, her lawyer, and hopefully Lane, here to provide a second statement on the prints on the gun. It wasn't exactly planned, but when the doctor called and said he wanted to come down to the station, Maro may have conveniently left out that they had a planned meeting with Ara. He'd been trying to connect the dots between the players in this case, and when the opportunity presented itself to see how they interact firsthand, he couldn't resist. Although a few steps behind, Maro and Ameno were rewarded by witnessing Ara heavily interrogating the doctor, who appeared uncharacteristically irritated.

"What did you tell them about me?" she demanded, one finger pointed in Dr. Dan's face. *She's like a rabid mouse,* Maro thought. *Tiny but fierce.*

This was better than they could have expected. It was clear that there were things Ara Hopkins did not want said to the police. Wanting to allow the conversation to continue but close enough to jump in if needed, Maro and Ameno leaned back on opposite sides of the doorway. Barry Goldberg, who was clearly late for the appointment, was going to be sorry he'd missed this confrontation.

Dan at first tried to shoulder past her, however, Ara juked her way back in front of him, not wanting to be ignored.

"What do you not want me to tell, Ara? That's the question."

"That may be the question for you, but I've already told the detectives everything I know. Even the stuff you think I wouldn't want anyone to know. All those secrets you've wanted me to keep all these years about you and me? I spilled every last detail to them."

Maro made a mental note of the choice in wording and the way Ara spit the sentence at him, almost as a threat. It didn't take a detective to fill the gap that there was more to their relationship than doctor and patient.

"So you filled them in on your new relationship with your stalker?"

With only a slight hesitation, Ara's tone switched gears from accusatory to innocent. "What are you talking about, Doctor? To my knowledge, I've never had a stalker."

"You know exactly who I am talking about. Your new boyfriend. Detective Bene. What a real gem he is. You see, I did have something to tell you the other night, something I'm sure you would have liked to hear first. Guess you should have hung around to listen, huh?"

Ara stomped, almost childlike, and was now even closer to the doctor's face than before.

"Maybe I would have *stuck around* if you hadn't tried to rape me. *Doctor*." She spit the last word out in disgust.

Before Maro and Ameno could even process what Ara had said, Dr. Dan lunged at her, gripping her shoulders so hard that she was practically lifted from the ground. Ameno raced to get in between the two but not before the doctor spat directly on Ara's face.

"You're a no-good whore!" he yelled as Ara raised her right knee to meet his center. The doctor hunched over as Ameno pulled Ara back toward the interrogation room and Maro contained Dr. Dan, reading him his rights. They'd figure out exactly what he was being charged with later. In less than perfect timing, Barry Goldberg appeared at the front door, rushing in as he realized the confrontation he was witnessing involved his client.

As if a switch had been flipped, Ara began wailing, holding her chest. Despite being stronger, Maro saw that Ameno was struggling to control her. Barry was demanding answers and Ara was sobbing, her face stained with a mix of mascara and Dan's spit. Scanning the rest of her body, Maro could already tell her arms would bruise where the doctor had grabbed her. *What a shit show.*

The porcelain doll the detective and lawyer were used to seeing had shattered. Ara held both hands around her stomach, retching and crying as her lawyer tried to calm her down. From the looks of it, Ara Hopkins had finally cracked.

CHAPTER 38

"Please tell me you had a stroke and lost control of your judgment. That you didn't actually think this through and decide it was a good idea." Hernandez had both detectives backed in the corner like beaten dogs, tails tucked tightly between their legs. Maro was hoping to get something from the planned interaction, but he never could have expected the dark turn it was going to take.

"It wasn't planned, Hernandez, it was just a horrible coincidence." Maro didn't feel right letting Ameno take the fall on this one. Though his arrogant partner could probably use a slap on the wrist, it had been Maro's idea and he knew it dallied with the line. But even he couldn't have expected what transpired, to his knowledge Ara and the doctor hadn't seen each other in years. How could he know that they had met up and worse, that an attempted sexual assault had taken place? Though he'd suspected the doctor was a creep since the first time he'd laid eyes on him.

"Coincidence? I wasn't born yesterday, Maro, and knowing you and your—what did you like to call it? Gut instinct?—I know this little meet up was orchestrated. Goldberg's going to go for blood. Your blood. Not mine. Got it? I'm not stepping in on this one, he can drag you through the streets, for all I care."

Maro shifted in his seat, trying to avoid the uncomfortable bite of being called out in front of his partner.

"Goldberg called us. Said Hopkins wanted to give another statement documenting certain events. We scheduled the interview, and that was that."

"And her old therapist, who allegedly tried to rape her just a day ago, happened to walk in the front door at the same time? Jesus Christ, you must really think I am a goddamn fool."

"If there was an attempted assault, why didn't Bene report it? And why was she meeting him off hours, at his home? Those are the questions you should be asking, Hernandez, and you know it." Maro stood, allowing the anger to bubble through his body. Ameno stood with him, showcasing a united front.

"Don't overstep here, Detective. I have my own questions I'm looking into when it comes to Bene and the validity of the rape claim. Either way, no more games, understand me? If you are going to get her,

242

you are going to get her the right way," she said, overly enunciating "the right way." Like most DAs, Martina Hernandez was a by-the-books kind of woman. If she could not use something to her advantage to win a case, then she didn't want to know about it. She stood, motioning for the door, saying, "Send Goldberg in, I'm sure he's hanging around out there waiting to chew my goddamn head off."

And he was. As soon as the door opened, Goldberg pushed past the detectives into the office.

"You mind telling me what the hell is going on here? Why is my client, a victim let me remind you, getting assaulted in the lobby when she comes to give a formal statement to help your god damn circus of a department?"

"A little respect, Barry? Are you forgetting I'm an attorney, just like yourself?"

"Let's knock off sexism, racism, whatever card you're trying to play to cover your ass today. I'm a Jew with a limp dick that needs Viagra, and you are no Jenny from the block with perky tits, we done with that, we cross out those lines?"

Martina would have hammered Maro if he ever spoke to her like that, but she just let Barry rant. "Barry, it was a coincidence. I'm sorry but it was a detail overlooked when scheduling. A mistake."

"Please, Martina, you can't even convince yourself this wasn't set up to knock my client off of her barely-there kilter." Barry threw a hefty file on the desk standing between the two. "Here's her statements. We also will be pursuing charges against Dr. Dan DaVadere for assault, as well as the witness intimidation, falsifying records, and harassment charges against this department."

"Intimidation? Now I think you're off your rocker. You and I both know that won't stick." Martina glared at Maro. He was going to pay for this one, despite the fact Goldberg was probably just blowing smoke.

She picked up the file and leafed through the documents noting, "Detective Bene's name seems to come up quite a bit here, huh? Odd timing considering their new relationship status."

"They are two adults who found comfort in each other after the untimely death of someone they both loved dearly," he said. "But grief does odd things to people. I'm sure a detail like that could be *overlooked*."

"Or this was a case of knocking off the one person who stood in their way."

"You say potato, I say patato." Despite the youthful remark, Martina and Maro both knew what he meant. Each could argue their side and paint whatever picture best suited the case they were spinning. They were both extremely gifted at their craft.

"If he loves her, as you say, why wouldn't he report the attempted sexual assault?"

"We're not pressing charges on the sexual assault, just what happened here today. There's a lot of history between Dr. D and my client. History neither party is trying to stir up for the sake of their own reputations. Therefore, no reason to report it." Maro and Martina exchanged knowing glances. Obviously, the doctor and his one-time patient did more than discuss coping skills in their hour-long sessions.

"Was it consensual then?" Martina asked.

"Who the hell knows? But there will be no charges other than those for your little charade today."

"We're booking the doctor for assault, Barry. He's in the process of being photographed and processed as we speak."

"Good, let's go talk to my client," Barry said, "And, Martina, you may want to tune into the news tonight. A little heads up, Ara will be making her first public statement."

Of course she is, Maro thought.

The detectives, accompanied by Martina and Barry, escorted Ara to an interview on the opposite side of the precinct from where Dan was being held. Lane had arrived just minutes after receiving the call from Barry. Shaken and bruised, Ara sat at the table next to Lane and across from the detectives. Each lawyer stood back, not wanting to overwhelm the interview.

As in the interviews prior, Maro leafed through his notebook finding a clean page before tapping the end of his pen. He dated the top right corner of the page and looked back up at Ara.

"I want to start by apologizing to you for what happened earlier. Despite your attorney's belief, it was not an intentional set up by our department. Your safety and mental well-being have been, and continue to be, a top priority for our team here and it is extremely important that you believe that and trust our department. We are the good guys."

Ara nodded looping her fingers through Lane's.

"It's also worth noting that we had no prior knowledge of a personal relationship between you and Dr. DaVadere or an attempted sexual assault. Obviously, our department would have investigated such accusations thoroughly if informed of these details." Maro did not attempt to hide his judging stare toward Lane. An old-school lawman, he could not understand why any decent detective would not report a crime of such scale to law enforcement.

Taking the bait, Lane interrupted, "Wasn't my idea, Maro. She didn't want to press charges, and I respected her wishes. If she wouldn't talk, there was no crime to report."

Interrupting, Ara said, "I do not want this to reflect poorly on Lane. He advised me to report it, and based on today I'm sure he's kicking himself for listening to me. Dan is far more dangerous than I thought and he has made it clear he has an unhealthy obsession with me."

Maro simply gave a *mmm hmmm* before continuing the interview, knowing that sometimes it was best not to over speak. He jotted a few gibberish notes before offering water to all in the room. After they declined, he continued.

"Goldberg told us you want to give another official statement on the gun used in your husband's murder. If you don't have any other questions for me, we can get on with it."

"None at this time."

"Do we have your permission to record this interview?" They weren't going to have any additional missteps today.

"Of course."

Barry and Martina each pressed start on their personal devices, obviously not wanting to miss a beat moving forward. The detectives adjusted the old-school recorder on the table before saying the necessary disclosure statements to get started. After a few basic questions, Maro asked Ara to explain again the specifics on the gun and why both her and Lane's fingerprints were found.

"Brad was becoming somewhat paranoid over the last few months. There were a few clients specifically who seemed to shake him up, as well as someone that was related to business he had with his father. I don't know names, or what type of business, his father was good at keeping me out of the loop with certain matters. Obviously, I now realize, he did not confide his secrets to me. Given his multiple affairs, I suppose he had others to exchange pillow talk with. But I knew he was worried."

"Mystery threats, seems convenient," Ameno said before being hushed by Hernandez.

"He was very secretive, Detective." Ara continued. "He wanted the gun for protection. Said he'd feel better having it. Lane and I were character witnesses for the application, along with, I believe, one other person from his office."

"All of this can be corroborated with the paperwork," Barry said, placing an envelope containing copies of the original documents filed on the table.

"Brad trusted Lane more than anyone, his opinion was very important to him. He was with us every step through purchasing the gun as well as at the range after to show us how to use it. Although the gun spent most of its time in a locked drawer, there were plenty of occasions for our prints to get on it."

Maro circled a note several times, digging the pen into the paper. He knew all of this already, he needed something new to spark movement in this case. His frustration with the unsolved case was growing, and he was quite frankly getting sick of the main characters.

"That's a very logical story, Ara, and thank you for sharing. There's just a few problems that seem to have no answer here. You see, I believe you, but then who did it? It's not a robbery, you said so yourself: the gun was locked away in a drawer. Someone had to know where the gun was, someone had to be able to get to it. And you want me to believe that all of this happened in a matter of minutes while you were conveniently off camera, hiking your pregnant self up multiple flights of stairs in heels?"

"We were out for an entire evening, Detective, and quite frankly I haven't seen that gun since Brad locked it away. I don't think Brad checked on it often either, though I can't be one hundred percent sure. Not that I'm trying to do your job here, but the gun could have been removed from the drawer at any time and we wouldn't have known."

"Fine, I agree someone could have been lying in wait in the apartment for you two to come back home, but why and who?" Maro loosened the tie around his neck suddenly feeling warm. "You seem like a nice woman, and I want to believe you that you had nothing to do with this, but you have to make me believe it, because right now there's not many other places to look."

Barry jumped from the sidelines and was at the table earning his high price retainer. "We've been nothing but cooperative. That ends if this badgering continues."

"Not badgering, Goldberg, take your panties out of their bunch. There's a goddamn piece missing here, and your client needs to start talking!"

"We've been talking. We just don't have the story you want to hear. Wouldn't be the first time you ruined an innocent victim's life by overreaching." Barry motioned to Ara that the interview was done and began to gather his things.

Hernandez interrupted, "Calm down, boys. We all have the same goal and it is to solve this case. We want closure for her, Barry, just like you."

"Closure, my ass. You want to persecute her and parade your victory for the politicians."

Ameno jumped into the conversation, saying, "It would be nothing short of predictable if she is covering for her boyfriend."

These two just can't get along, Maro thought, preparing for what was sure to be another blowout between the two younger detectives.

"Bullshit!" Lane said. "You know damn well I was working. My captain gave you his statement. What else do you want from me?"

"I still think you got there a little fast, Bene!" Ameno chimed.

"Brad was sleeping with half the town, with my goddamn stepsister. Plenty of people had a reason to kill him!" Ara shouted.

The room fell silent as the attention snapped back to her. Ara's leg shook slightly from nerves but her face showed no sign of it.

"Lane and Brad were like brothers. I'd just received the happiest of news, finding out I was pregnant. Neither of us wanted Brad dead, you will see tonight in my interview, I had accepted him and wanted to move forward with my family." Ara looked to Lane and took a deep breath. "There is more that you need to know."

Hopefully something that leads somewhere, Maro thought before motioning for her to continue.

"Dr. DaVedere and I were involved in a sexual relationship for about a decade," she paused, leaving Maro on the edge of his seats and doing the math in his head. "Since I was seventeen years old, up until my marriage to Brad."

Maro noticed Lane looked as if he might be sick, he had opened his mouth but no words came out.

"Dr. Dan can be very manipulative; he knows how to act to get what he wants. His ego. It's everything to him."

"Damn his ego!" Lane banged the table.

Maro, not entirely shocked by the new allegations was willing to say what everyone else was thinking. "These are very serious accusations, Ara."

Ara nodded. "I'd imagine banging your seventeen-year-old patient would be quite serious."

"Jesus, Ara, don't speak like that." Lane was visibly shaken.

"What do you want me to say, that it didn't happen? 'Cause it did and I am so sorry, but I was a kid. My dad had just passed away and all I had was Arabelle. I was looking for love and thought I had found it by having sex with him."

"It's not *sex*. It's statutory rape," Lane said.

But Ara looked directly back toward Maro and his partner. "It wasn't forced. Wrong, yes. But not forced. Plus, it was over ten years ago, isn't there some sort of statute of limitations or something like that?"

Maro cleared his throat. "Age of consent is seventeen in New York, doesn't mean he's not a no-good creep, though." Hernandez simply nodded in confirmation.

Ara continued, "It is in the past and I would never have brought it up, but I want you to know the extent of our relationship so you could see why the doctor would want to harm me, possibly even Brad."

"You and Mr. Bugia started dating when you were twenty-five years old, correct?" Maro asked, taking bulleted notes to build out a timeline.

"Yes."

"And your relationship with Dr. DaVadere began when you were seventeen."

"Correct."

"Were you having intimate relationships with both men for a time?"

"For some time, yes. In the beginning, I wasn't sure where things were going, and I was comfortable with Dan. Brad also was out a lot of nights, so maybe it was just out of boredom. But I called it off right after we got engaged and was ready to commit fully to Brad."

Maro nodded, tossing his notes to the table. "You suppose you were the only patient?"

"During that time, I believe I was. I couldn't speak for him now. Up until recently, we hadn't spoken for a few years. He didn't exactly take it well when I broke things off. I'm afraid he really grew to hate me after that. And to hate Brad."

Maro was thoroughly satisfied that his initial feelings on the doctor were spot on. Not only was he potentially a child molester, based on what Ara was saying, he seemed to have an unhealthy obsession with her and their victim. They'd have to look in to the doc more, but where he stood now, it was looking like he had a motive.

"There's one other thing, I'm not sure I could prove it, which is why I haven't mentioned it until now, but I think the doctor had been following me. Brad and I would be out somewhere, dinner or something, and I'd think I'd catch a glimpse of him, but when I would turn to look, he wouldn't be there."

"But you have no proof of this, just what you *think* you saw?"

Ara's eyes squinted, her face tightening defensively. "No. I said I couldn't prove it. But I could never really shake the feeling that we were being watched."

After a few more questions, Ara signed a written statement, reiterating that anything Dr. Dan said about her or Lane could not be trusted, and that she truly believed if she wasn't happy with him, he didn't want her happy with anyone.

"Thank you again for your cooperation," Ameno said as Lane and Ara exited with Barry. Hernandez exchanged a stern look with both detectives.

"This is big, Maro, may even be your guy. I suggest you start exploring these other leads." She turned and exited as well, leaving no time for him to argue.

Ameno quickly followed, shouting, "Hey, Bene! A word?"

Great, can't he give this up? Maro motioned for Ameno to bring the conversation back into the room. Martina would hand it to him if he allowed another outburst today.

Lane looked to Ara, who nodded. He returned to the interview room and closed the door behind him.

"I'd like to get on better ground, us and you. We are brothers in blue, after all," Ameno said. "I can't help but feel some tension between us."

Maro couldn't hold in his laugh, as Ameno waited for a response from Lane but got nothing. "But it's unnecessary. And if I have to be the bigger man, I will."

"See that's my problem, brother. The bigger man shit. You seem to think you have a strong handle on the case," Lane finally said.

"Don't we?" Ameno asked.

"I don't really know what you think you know. What I do know is that even after everything you just heard about the doc, you are still humping my leg hoping to get something out of me."

Ameno chuckled. "Fair enough," he said. "That's all a great story with good old Dr. Dan, but at the end of the day you're the one sleeping with her and we've got your prints on the murder weapon."

Lane offered no response. Ameno leaned in and said, "And I'm sitting back thinking, this whole thing could have been planned."

Lane took a step forward. "If I were you, I'd be looking into that lunatic doctor. Dig deeper, I'm not your man," he said before pulling the door open.

Before he could leave the room, Maro spoke up, "Let's say you did do it, would she be worth all this?"

Lane stopped but didn't turn around and said, "Is anyone worth killing another person?"

I guess that depends, Maro thought.

He and Ameno sat silently after Lane left, considering the new circumstances.

"The doctor did always give me the freaking creeps," he finally said, slicing through the silence.

"Do you really believe her? Seems a little convenient at this point."

"It'd be a hell of a thing to lie about. Especially in front of her new boyfriend like that."

This was the part of the job that Maro loved best. Ara Hopkins had just breathed some life into what was looking to be his first unsolved case since cleaning up his act.

"Call his office, let's see what else we can dig up on the doc."

CHAPTER 39

The bright beams cascading on to her from all directions reminded her of searchlights. The production crew assured her the stage lighting would make her appear warm, appealing even, but Ara was positive it was more along the lines of sweaty and discombobulated. She could feel her expensive department store makeup beginning to melt into the creases of her skin. The onset team brushed her face with toners and highlighters, enhancing her cheekbones and brow while producers briefed her with sample questions before ultimately admitting the interview could turn in a different direction on the fly if the host saw an opportunity.

"That's what Shirley does best," they said matter-of-factly even as they swore her best interest, not the show's, was what was most important to their host. "America will cry for you and your heartache when you're through today." *Or convict me of murder and crucify me on social media*, Ara thought.

Shirley Stapleton, a former prosecutor turned television host, had a personality as big as her Texas hair. She was known to be hard-hitting and had a knack for sensational commentary on some of the country's top criminal cases. If there was a crime show to be on, it was Shirley's.

Raina appeared much more comfortable getting dolled up, even dallying with a few of the crew members as they fussed with her hair. Ara wasn't entirely sure she would agree to going on air with her, but with Arabelle backing the choice, she knew eventually Raina would cave to the opportunity to be in the limelight.

She never stops. Ara watched Raina tilt her head and giggle as she meandered easily through the prep, jealous of the fact that she always seemed to be *on*.

"Thanks for doing this with me," Ara said. "Means a lot."

"Of course, Ara, I would do anything for you." To which the producers clasped their hands into a fraudulent series of "Aws!"

The executive producer had been more than happy to agree to Ara's request to have Raina accompany her on the show. They couldn't pass on an opportunity to capture the side of the story many were waiting to hear. After some rescheduling by the network, the sisters were slotted to appear during a prime-time segment.

The producers showed the two women to their seats on a platform a foot or so off of the ground. Ara would sit next to Shirley, with a comfortable space between them, while Raina sat off to Ara's right.

Lane and Barry kindly offered their support from behind the stage crew who buzzed about setting up the wired microphone clipped at Ara's collar. Through the chaos, Lane offered Ara a halfhearted smile, which she was glad to return with more enthusiasm. He hadn't spoken a single word to her about her relationship with Dr. Dan, but she could tell he was still working through how he felt about it. She lifted her hand and waved, smiling again, before returning her attention to the set crew.

Shirley came out moments later and approached the two women. She was everything Ara thought she would be, right down to her firm handshake. Ara fumbled to stand in the form-fitting black dress Barry had provided for her to wear during the segment.

"Ara," Shirley said, confidently extending her hand to touch hers, "I want to start first by offering not only my extreme condolences for your husband's murder, but promising this interview will only aid in bringing more awareness to the case, and personalizing your story. I would also like to assure you that I will extend every effort on my team to bring you and your family justice."

Ara noted the alarming similarity between *bring you justice* and *bring you to justice*. Thank God this wasn't a live segment. Although allowing professionals to snip and trim behind the scenes until they cultured up the right amount of drama seemed potentially worse.

"Thank you. I know you work tirelessly at helping solve these sorts of cases, and I am honored that you're interested in telling my story."

Ara's anxiety was interrupted by the same producer who had prepped her during hair and makeup. "Remember, this is a forum for you to show the world what you want them to understand about you and your relationship with your husband. You are free to decline questions and to pause the interview at any time if it becomes overwhelming. But remember your audience. You need to open up and show them why you are here. Show them you are innocent."

I will show them exactly what they need to see. Nodding her head, Ara sat back in her seat, unable to shake the thought that this was probably how the conversations between Shirley and Congressman

Bugia started also. Shirley and Raina went through the same formalities before taking their places.

Her ears continued to hum with the familiar tune of blood rushing to her head. She was sure by now her makeup looked as if a preschooler had applied it with finger paint as she gently dabbed her forehead with the supplied Kleenex.

"For when you cry," the set dresser had told her reassuringly. Ara supposed everyone cried; some with false tears, others genuine, but surely everyone cried.

Shirley's hand touched Ara's and again she returned to reality, awkwardly realizing that she had missed the entire opening segment. Repeating herself in her concerned voice, Shirley prompted Ara to tell the viewers about Brad. Ara gripped the arm of the chair tightly, using it as a stress ball to focus her nervous attention to.

"My husband was everything to me." Her eyes focused on Barry. He'd made her promise to nail the interview, and she'd already slipped up. Turning her attention to Shirley, she said, "He could make you laugh while washing the dishes and turn a flop of a fundraising event into a success, all without loosening his tie. Loving him was easy."

Lane withdrew back into the off-camera darkness as she continued, "Everyone enjoyed being around him. He was one of those extraordinary men who made you love yourself more when around him. Brad had a way of making you feel special." She made sure to speak slowly, hoping to pass off her lies as the truth.

"Sounds like the perfect gentleman!" Shirley said, nodding. "But you've learned a little more about your husband since his passing, correct?"

"No matter what I learned, I know I loved him very deeply, and he loved me. We were lucky to have each other, even if things weren't perfect in our marriage. Brad never acted without thinking, he made every move in life with intention. I am sure there was a reason for the things he did."

"Until that dreadful night," Shirley led.

"Yes, until that terrible night."

"I think most agree there seems to be some big holes in the story of what happened. Is there anything you can tell us here tonight to help address those?"

Ara nodded and searched beyond the cameras for any signal from Barry, unfortunately, thanks to the lighting, she would have to continue on her own.

"I wish I could make better sense of it myself, honestly. It all seemed to happen so fast. We were out celebrating a recent victory Brad had at work. I had recently found out that I was pregnant and thought it would the perfect time to tell him, but when we got to the restaurant Brad said he had a surprise of his own for me later that night. I felt guilty bursting his bubble and decided it would be best to wait to tell him my news."

"This is why you waited in the car, correct? Because he had a surprise?"

"Yes. Brad told me to wait for ten minutes or so before coming upstairs. It was cold, and I was anxious in the car. I knew he would be happy with the news of becoming a father, but I couldn't think of what he wanted to surprise me with. I couldn't help feeling like it was a trap, like somehow instinctively I knew something bad was happening." Pausing, Ara took a single breath before continuing. "It wasn't that weird that I took the stairs, I did it sometimes if I was stressed from a

266

day at work or something. I found it gave me time to unwind. From my understanding, there are no cameras that would capture me in the stairs, but I believe there is footage of me walking from that direction to our door and there is also the pedometer on my phone."

"Even so, Ara, that doesn't necessarily explain what happened once you entered the apartment," Shirley said, slightly stirring the pot.

"When I entered the apartment my whole world collapsed around me. Brad was on the floor, and there was so much blood. I remember seeing the gun on the floor and the blood coming from his chest. I knew he was dead."

"You would never learn what his surprise was, and he would never know he was going to be a father."

Ara felt the well-timed tears build. "No, I will never know."

After finishing her version of the events, Shirley cut to the chase, saying, "Things were not as perfect as they appeared in his life. Someone wanted him dead."

"To this day, I can't imagine someone who would want to hurt him, hurt us, in that manner."

"I have to note here that you said 'hurt us.'"

"Yes, us. My life ended that night with his. He would never know the news I was going to share or that we were going to be starting a family."

Raina reached over to Ara and squeezed her arm, which Ara returned with a simple smile. Shirley turned her attention to Raina, a now second-time guest on the show.

"Raina, you knew Ara and Brad better than most. Is there any scenario you could even consider where Ara had something to do with her husband's death?"

Ara swallowed the lump building in her throat.

"You didn't need to know them well to know that it wasn't an option. Their relationship was the kind you hoped for a best friend and sister. Their dedication to each other was inspiring."

"It's been pretty well documented that Brad was not faithful. Most would not feel inspired by that type of betrayal in something as sacred as marriage."

Ara pulled her hand away from Raina and adjusted her seating. "The world wants to believe we had secrets, but we did not. Brad and I had an honest understanding of where we both were in our lives and who we were spending time with. Even if it was unconventional."

Pausing, Ara turned to the camera. The lights caught a shimmering trickle of a tear building in the corner of her eye.

"While I'm not expecting everyone to understand our situation, I do think people can relate to it in some way. I was pregnant and we were finally going to have a family, something that Brad wanted more than any pleasures he was seeking outside of our marriage. I know Brad was not faithful, but our love ran much deeper than any physical indiscretion he had. When two people are as open as we were with each other, forgiveness and love always win."

What she was saying may not have been entirely true, but it also was not a complete and utter lie. In many ways, Ara had come to terms with who Brad was, after his death. Prior to that—what she'd actually known about or been comfortable with before his death—was another story.

Raina's breezy appearance had shifted. Her face now bore a forced grin as Ara and Shirley continued with the racy details of Brad's extramarital affairs. Raina seemed to be having trouble swallowing, looking increasingly uncomfortable next to an outwardly calm Ara.

It didn't go unnoticed by the professionals. Shirley asked Raina if everything was OK.

Raina sputtered, "It is just crushing to learn details like this about someone like Brad, someone I trusted to care for my sister. Every time I hear something he did to her, I could . . ."

This time, Ara placed her hand on Raina's knee. "Yes. Betrayal can be a tough pill to swallow." She then pulled Raina into her, holding her close, but in a way that ensured Raina's expression was left exposed to the camera. She looked as if she might throw up.

After releasing Raina, Ara said, "I am lucky I have such a great support system of friends. Without them, I am not sure how I could have survived after suffering such a blow," Ara continued.

A silence hushed the studio. Finally, the executive producer cleared her throat, moving the interview along. A half hour later the team said they had plenty for the segment and politely assured Ara and Barry that they would adhere to the preaddressed agreement when editing. The team assured Barry no statements would be used out of

270

order, or in incomplete fragments to create a different story. Shirley thanked the women before exiting. From across the studio, Ara saw Lane and nodded at him. Raina called her name as Ara walked away from the platform.

"I'm sorry, Ara," she said.

"For what?"

"I guess I didn't know all of the details about Brad's affairs. It's just . . . so sad for you."

"Sad," Ara repeated. "That is one way to look at it."

Raina shook her head in agreement as they shared a lips-only smile.

CHAPTER 40

At first, Ara hadn't even wanted to watch the completed interview, certain it would be too difficult, but Lane finally persuaded her it would be good to see how the world was now going to see her.

He picked up their favorite, pizza and red wine, and they picnicked on the living room floor. Lane had learned patience was not a trait Ara carried well, so he persuaded her to wait long enough so they would be able to fast forward through the DVR recording, avoiding any breaks or commercials. He wanted to get through this as quickly as possible. When the interview started, he offered up sweet compliments on the insignificant matters to ease the growing apprehension steaming through Ara's pores.

Ara appeared very natural on screen. Then there it was. As she'd eloquently meandered through Brad's infidelities, Lane noticed Raina appeared queasy and off-kilter. The TV crew hadn't missed it either; they had a knack for finding the drama. And in this case, drama was an understatement. Ara was casting herself free of the burden that came with being a woman scorned, while Raina appeared flush with guilt.

272

It was in that precise moment when Ara turned the interview that he knew she knew about Raina and Brad. Lane had tried to come up with a way to ask Ara what she knew about them ever since Maro and Ameno had conveniently leaked the secret, but if she hadn't known, he didn't want to be the one to tell her. *Why Raina, Brad? Why dig the knife even deeper into Ara?* Could Brad have wanted to strike Ara where it would cause the most damage?

Now the burning questions he had for his best friend could never be answered and at this point he didn't mind it that way. Some deeds were not deserving of an explanation. Especially from a word slinger like Brad.

On screen, the sisters were in what could have been perceived as a warm embrace. But the cameraman zoomed in on Raina's face, highlighting her tense jawbone. Now, sitting with pretzel legs and two hands gripping her wine glass, Ara was glued to the screen.

Not only did Ara know what Raina had done, she had made her move against her by manipulating the interview and leaving the world tidbits of betrayal to run with. Instead of revealing all the eggs in her basket for all to see, she allowed just a glimpse of the truth, letting the rumors explode like wild fire on social media until it engulfed all parties involved. Burning them to a crisp. Certainly, the rumors could be no worse than the entirety of the truth.

Lane's body ticked with a reaction the world would share. He wanted to cover her eyes, guard her from her sister and husband's betrayal, but instead he kissed her right cheek, determined to bring a sense of peace to her broken heart.

After an extended breath, Ara wrapped both arms around Lane, resting her right ear on his chest. His heart nearly beating out of his chest from the pure adrenaline pumping through his veins.

"Oscar-worthy performance, Ara Hopkins."

Letting go of his torso, she pushed the hair from her shoulders.

"I'm so sorry, Ara."

A single tear broke free and fell from her face, splashing onto her thigh.

"You didn't deserve this, baby, he should have just let you go. Divorced you. Anything would have been better than this."

"Maybe I do deserve every last bit of this for being so foolish," she said without breaking her stare, allowing more tears to trace paths through her cheeks.

"I was blind to everything, Lane, because I didn't want to admit it," Ara said, "He should have never married me, he was never happy. I deserve all of this because deep down, I knew it wasn't what he wanted. It was what his father wanted, he's the one that pushed Brad to check all the boxes: happy wife, home, and life. I knew Brad didn't want all that, but I didn't want to accept it. I was insecure, and checking boxes with him was easier than being alone."

Lane clumsily wiped her tears, as if he could catch each one and put it back. "No. You didn't. I won't sit back and let them do that to you. You said it yourself: his lies, his sins, that's what killed him. They all caught up with him. A person can't get away with living a life that's a lie forever. The world somehow catches up, but you would have never hurt him, you loved him."

Ara let her lips linger on her glass, taking a long-drawn sip before saying, "I don't even know that I did love him anymore, Lane. I thought I did, but I have no idea about anything now."

Shaking his head, Lane took the glass from her hands and placed it behind her on the end table.

"Just know that I am here now and that I will never hurt you the way he did. *Brad* was a fool, not you, for believing he was a good man. You wanted so badly to believe in his good side, and I did, too, but as we both know now, that was only a small part of him."

He scooped her up, trying to undo the damage his friend had bestowed on her life, and laid her back on the fleece set out under them, swept the hair from her face, and kissed her, hard, as if he had something to prove for the both of them.

"You never deserved this to happen to you," he said, tracing her jawline with the back of his fingers.

Lying behind her, looking over her shoulder, he watched as a transformation took place in Ara, her body relaxing as they finished watching the interview, a change from the overall depression that had hung above Ara like a cloud, to an even deeper sorrow. Looking down, Lane saw a woman who wanted to believe in so much good in the world, and it bothered him to know the people closest to her had not only let her down but had gutted her, leaving her insides exposed. After this interview, everyone would assume that she got burned not only by her husband, but her stepsister, too. It was a play she had to make, but Lane knew she didn't like it.

CHAPTER 41

For once Ara's plan played out perfectly: Raina was cast into a cloud of suspicion and the heat would be lifted, slightly, from her. Even if some still thought she did it, now she had a reason most could understand. Not many men would sleep with their wife's stepsister and friend, but Brad Bugia did.

After the interview, she couldn't even let Lane touch her, she needed space to process what she had started. Brad's father and his team were most likely already plotting how to control the damage, scheming how to tuck his son's sins and shortcomings back into a pretty box. Her own mother finally gave up after she ignored six of her calls. She would deal with Arabelle tomorrow.

Lane finally allowed himself to fall asleep sometime after 2 a.m., and he was breathing shallowly next to her in bed. It was now 6 a.m. and his alarm would be going off any minute for work. Rolling toward him, she put her head on his chest.

"Did you fall asleep at all?" he said as he wrapped both arms around her.

278

"No."

She moved back to her side so they were face-to-face. Leaning
in, she let Lane kiss her, dragging her hand to just above the elastic of
his boxer briefs. He undid her button-down pajama shirt, revealing a
bare chest. Now skin to skin, suddenly needing to feel him, their
embrace felt desperate but right.

He moved on top of her and kissed her chest, then neck, savoring
each. Nibbling slightly at her ear before coming back to her lips.

"Are you OK?"

Ara pushed his now longer dingy blonde hair from his eyes and
shook her head yes.

Smiling a knowing, boyish grin, he kissed her, delicately cupping
one of her breasts in his hand as she opened her legs, feeling his length
pressing into her.

Sex was sex. At least that's how it had been since her first time
when the emotion was stripped from the act in Dan's office. Sure she
always enjoyed it, but she was often left numb from the void of true
intention. As Lane moved on top of her, every one of her nerve endings
danced with an unfamiliar zest. She wanted him inside her and to feel

what could never be said through words. In some form, the secret was out. Raina and Brad committed the ultimate betrayal, and knowing that the world would know made letting it go easier. Many times throughout their relationship, she would assure herself that she really did love Brad and that marriages weren't easy or perfect.

But here with Lane, basking in the early morning sunlight that poured in from the window, she felt something different.

Her hands pushed him deeper into her. She let her entire body release, leading to a feeling of true pleasure. As her body tightened, Lane came before collapsing on top of her leaving each gasping for their breath.

"I love you, Ara."

Her body trembled slightly as she turned on her side, bringing her knees up to her chest, suddenly feeling vulnerable. After years of keeping everything in, the past forty-eight hours had been a rollercoaster of emotions for her. Curled up in the most innocent of positions, Lane held her.

"Things could get worse before they get better, Lane."

"I know."

"If you love me, promise you will be here no matter what."

Lane rolled over and swung his feet to stand from the bed.

Leaning down he kissed her forehead and said, "Promise, promise."

CHAPTER 42

The banging on the door was relentless. The building's board would be sending a letter in the next few days complaining of the commotion. *God damn prudes.*

Dan weaved his way over to answer it, his gut burning from the afterthought of five bourbons on an empty stomach. He was always a lousy drunk but after everything that happened with him and Ara, he'd needed to feel numb. The bourbon a perfect solution. The peephole revealed the last person he wanted to see standing in his hallway. After debating whether to answer, the insistent pounding forced him to unhinge the chain and unbolt the lock.

Raina looked equally as inebriated, maybe more: shaky on her elevator heels, lipstick staining the area under her bottom lip. Her normally cheap debonair look seemed helplessly flawed as she popped her hip out from habit.

"What are you doing here?"

"I'm sorry, I shouldn't have just showed up. I couldn't think of anywhere else to go."

Go home, you're pathetic, he thought, unpersuaded by her wasted attempts at puppy dog eyes.

"It's late, I'm not sure I'm in the mood, Raina."

"I've had a really bad day," she said, anxiously looking over her shoulder back toward the elevators, "and I don't know what's going to happen to me, and you were the only person I could think of who had any reason to miss me."

Miss you? He could have laughed right there in her face at the thought. But the cloudiness plaguing his brain had begun to dissipate, and he decided there may be an upside to inviting her in and playing out their fake romance for one more night. Other than an easy blow job. Unbeknownst to her, he knew exactly why she was so wasted. He had seen the interview with Shirley Stapleton, it was only a matter of time before the entire truth came out. Based on her current inebriated state, maybe she would have more to say that he could use to help Ara. Or at least get back in her good graces.

Raina bumped into the walls as she walked down the corridor, reaching the wet bar and pouring herself an unnecessary splash of his fifteen-year-old Pappy Van Winkle. Nodding to her in agreement, Raina poured a second fat pour and handed him the glass before falling back onto the sofa with exaggerated exhaustion.

"Life's a bitch. Or she's a bitch, I don't even know anymore." She sighed, swirling her glass. "I'm a bitch."

Dan's hands tightened, pressing his prints deep into the tumbler. Having to listen to her nonsense was going to be harder than he thought. He should hate Ara right now, but, of course, he didn't. He was booked on simple assault charges and probably would get off with a fine if she even pursued it. All in all, the damage would be minimal.

"She is always ruining everything for me. Making me look like shit. I'm not a shit!"

He hushed her. Despite his building being advertised as sound proof, it was New York City. The walls vibrated with the lives of your neighbors. "Do you mind enlightening me on who we are talking about?"

"My stuck-up bitch of a stepsister. The one whose husband was murdered." Raina's words were now slurring almost beyond comprehension but she continued, "Who am I kidding, she probably did it. I can't even say I'd blame her given what she found out about him."

284

Jumping to his feet, Dan caught himself before grabbing Raina by the throat and launching her off the fire escape. He had to be cool.

"You should be careful with accusations like that. Spitting out lies could damage a lot of people. Yourself included."

"Did you see what Shirley freaking Stapleton and her drama horny geek squad did to the interview?" She clearly hadn't heard a word he said.

Dan sipped the bourbon, allowing it to linger in his mouth longer than usual as he considered the woman sitting in front of him: narcissistic, self-serving, sleeping her way through her insecurities.

"Why would I have seen an interview conducted by Shirley Stapleton? Shows like that are meant to stir drama, infuriate the audience. I'm surprised you even agreed to go on."

"I don't know, because I asked you to watch? Arabelle, Barry, they all thought it was a good idea to help Ara. So, of course, what do I do, I agree and play along. Now I am going to be the one that looks like shit." Spittle leaped from Raina's lips, spraying Dan. "I probably won't even be able to leave my goddamn house." Withdrawing to a childlike pout, she swirled her drink, watching closely as it spun around and around the glass.

It's all about you. "People can see through the nonsense."

"I had an affair with my sister's husband, and now he's dead. People are going to see me for exactly what I am."

Playing the part, Dan stepped in between Raina's spread legs and lifted her chin, smiling as comfortingly as he could stomach. "That is pretty bad," he said. "But half this city is sleeping with each other. Trust me, people will get over it."

"Not when the cheater is a congressman's son who was murdered! If things had just gone as planned, none of this would have happened, but no, Brad was weak, saw the test, and crumbled to his knees."

"What test, Raina? What plan?"

She gulped back her drink, retching at the burn. Standing, she seesawed to the back bedroom, sloshing what was left of her drink on the comforter as she sat on the bed. Dan rushed over, taking the glass before any more damage could be done to his luxury duvet. "What are you talking about, Raina?"

"I am talking about you," she said, awkwardly bopping his nose with her pointer finger. She spread her legs, revealing a sheer black thong, touching herself with the same hand she'd nearly poked his eye out with. "And how you are going to kiss me. Here." Gently, she massaged herself, moving her tongue to her upper lip. If he wasn't wasted, this raunchy scene would have been unbearable. Luckily, a night of heavy boozing purged the blood through his veins.

"Tell me what test first."

Laughing. "The pregnancy test. We had a plan, him and me, but then he saw that freaking test in the trash and he caved like a little bitch. And now he's freaking dead, Ara knows everything, and I'm screwed." He twirled her around, forcing her face down on the bed. He unbuckled his pants, then lifted her skirt and moved her teaser thong to the left and pushed himself inside her.

Positive she was guilty of committing more than one heinous betrayal to Ara, Dr. Dan grabbed a fistful of her hair, wrapping it around his hand and wrist, arching her back as he pulled, taking her from behind. Raina was dirty in every sense of the word.

When they were done, he flattened onto the bed next to her, gasping for air.

"Glad I came by? Sounded like you needed that." She moved her head up to the pillow, turning to her back, leaving her skirt disheveled up at her waist.

Sighing, he moved up to his side of the bed. "You bet. Let me grab you a night cap."

Moments later, he returned with a refilled glass, this time with an added shot of Ambien. Not that she needed it. She practically drugged herself prior to her arrival, but he needed her out cold.

She gulped down the drink in a single shot before snuggling back onto the pillows, her breath deepening to a hum.

Dan finished the remainder of his own cocktail; liquid courage couldn't hurt right now. He adjusted her panties and pulled her skirt back down to cover her bare ass.

Halfway through, he decided she needed to pay for what she did to Ara. First he placed one hand around her throat, pushing slightly, but the stiffness of her neck repulsed him. Growing up in rural America, he was the only child on his street that hated killing bugs. The crunching noise their pathetic frames made when the life was removed made him cringe. Imagining the sensation on a human made his skin crawl.

Standing back, he wondered why couldn't she just die on her own, overdose on the cocktail of "I messed up" feel betters? For years, he watched as she infiltrated Ara and Brad's life. It was calculated and strategic. She clearly wanted to hurt her stepsister and for a smart man, Brad Bugia sure could be stupid. Ara was so innocent, so unaware, never noticing the treachery surrounding her in those she loved.

Lunging for his feather pillow, Dan pushed down on Raina's face with all of his strength, but no matter how hard he pushed her stomach continued to rise and fall with life.

Disgusted, Dan sat back against the wall, head in hands. Apparently, he was a monster, just not the type that could kill. The booze hit him like a lightning bolt, sending him up to the bed. He pushed the pillow off Raina's face, wrapping an arm around her, he whispered into her ear, "I will make sure you get yours, I promise," before nodding off into a deep, hazy sleep.

***

Harley sat in the lobby, waiting for the mysterious woman to return from the elevator. The night guard glanced over every five minutes or so, most likely debating whether or not a barely five foot, properly-dressed woman was considered a threat.

Harley fed him a line earlier about waiting on a boyfriend, but as the clock ticked, the guard's suspicions rose.

"You a rockette?"

Her questioning look was reciprocated with the security guard's plump finger pointing at her tapping high heels. She hadn't noticed the nervous melody prior.

"Do I look like I'm five ten?" she snarled.

"I hear the ones on the end of the lines only have to be five six."

Moron. "I'm only five foot. Sorry, I'll stop the tapping."

The night guard shrugged and went back to flipping through an outdated *Sports Illustrated*.

Harley grabbed her purse and marched to the elevator. This squatty troll wouldn't stand in her way. Moments later, she used a spare key to enter Dr. Dan's apartment.

The spare key he kept at the office was meant for emergencies only but it didn't stop her from sneaking over when she knew he was out of town. She'd run a bath, pour herself a glass of cheap red he wouldn't notice opened, and fantasize about a life they would share. A future she was certain of, until a few months ago when the doctor began to distance himself. At first she was nothing short of supportive. Bringing him tea, rubbing his shoulders, letting him take out his stress by having her heartless and hard against his desk. But the tension never left his body, and she was left bitten with abandonment. His heart was bleeding for another, she could tell.

The television was still blaring, and the lights were all on. The apartment looked more disheveled then she'd seen it before. Stepping out of her heels, she crept toward the bedroom. She closed her eyes tight before pushing open the door to his bedroom. Naked, his arm flung around the mystery woman. Stunned and indignant, anger erupted through Harley's body.

In just three small steps, she was standing next to them, watching as their stomachs rose and fell in unison. She kissed her middle finger before brushing it against Dan's bare arm, watching a few hairs rise on his neck before she slowly turned to leave.

When she got to the hallway her pace quickened, and by the time she was out of the elevator, she was in a full on sprint. Racing past the guard, she pushed through the revolving door, the cool air whipping at her face.

"I love your wild side. Crazy and beautiful go hand in hand," the doctor used to say as she sat with arms crossed on the couch, guarding herself as she was brought up to do.

He'd touch her upper thigh and kiss her neck, whispering sweet taunts, how she was free to show him who she wanted to be. Back then he wanted to see her crazy. And now he would.

CHAPTER 43

"How could you be so stupid?"

Ara picked at her cuticles, choosing anything over eye contact with her mother.

"Answer me, Ara. Is that what you intended when you brought Raina on Shirley Stapleton with you, make our family look like a bunch of hillbillies?"

"Do I have to remind you that you were there when we made the decision?" Ara knew her mother was furious that her high-paid attorney had a role in masterminding a move she now viewed as such a dreadful mistake.

"You put a match to some very ugly opinions. They are going to roast your sister over an open flame." Arabelle shared Raina's flare for dramatics.

"Stepsister. Plus, how was I supposed to know Raina would react like that? We'd hardly spoken until you intruded in my business as usual and made me apologize to her. Obviously, she was avoiding me for certain reasons."

"You threw her under the bus. There's not a dusting of truth to that affair between her and Brad; I would have known about it."

Ara's laughter could no longer be contained. Typical of her mother to not see the obvious, turning a blind eye when she wanted. "You would have? How? We hardly even speak. Unless, of course, your little minion Raina would have told you."

"You are losing control of this situation. Brad wasn't perfect, but he was a good partner. Look at what they are saying about him now. You are turning your marriage into tabloid trash."

Sometimes it was easier not to fight. "You don't know anything about our marriage, Mother. You weren't even sober at the damn ceremony."

Arabelle walked to the window, pulling a pack of Marlboro Menthols from her Chanel clutch, a habit Ara thought she'd kicked years ago. *Guess drinking isn't her only vice.* "What is wrong with this thing?" she asked, fighting with the window before realizing it could only be opened about an inch.

"They only open a crack."

Her mother looked back blankly.

"They don't want you jumping out and knocking out a poor pedestrian on your way down."

Mumbling a slew of cuss words under her breath, Arabelle shut the window and walked to the door, stopping before opening it.

"I am tired of this childish competition between you and her. Peter and I tried to always make the best decisions for both of you. Obviously he is furious with you now, but we always treated you two equally."

Ara needed this conversation to be over. "Keep telling yourself that. I'm not apologizing again to her, and I'm sure as hell not going to support her publicly. If that is what you are here for, do us both a favor and save us the time of an argument and leave."

Arabelle smirked and turned, leaving her alone in her apartment.

"Dammit!" Ara screamed out loud, her mother had the worst timing.

Lane hadn't answered a call or text from her all day. She was sure after having time to think, he was disgusted with her for sleeping with Dr. Dan. With everything happening with the interview, they hadn't had a chance to talk about it.

When her call went to voicemail for the third time, Ara could feel her anxiety building. The last thing she wanted was for Lane to be angry with her. Kicking herself, she wished she'd told him the whole story after he showed up at Dan's apartment, instead of blindsiding him in front of the detectives. Even though he didn't have much to say after the interview, he did just make love to her that morning like they never had before . . . . Maybe she was being irrational, but he never went this long without checking in.

You've reached Detective Lane Bene . . .

Frustrated, she clicked into her text messages. *Nothing.*

Desperate pleas alternated in her head: *Please don't hate me, please pick up.*

Lane gave her something Brad never could, selfless love, and now she was at risk of losing it all because of Dr. Dan. Did she really ruin the one good thing that came from this nightmare?

CHAPTER 44

Driving across the river and uptown, Maro repeated everything they had on the doctor out loud to Ameno. Any manipulation of a doctor-patient relationship was sickening, but to breach that boundary with a seventeen-year-old girl who'd just lost her father was unfathomable. Sick or not, though, it didn't prove murder. If they were really going to nail the son-of-a-bitch, they needed something more to build their case on.

The doctor's office was quiet for midday. The afternoon time slots typically booked with housewives, fitting their appointments between Pilates and lunch dates. Scanning the empty reception room, Ameno turned the appointment book around so he could read the notes, noting the time had been blocked off. A television on the far wall played the *Ellen DeGeneres Show*, while a second TV adjacent read the news through closed captioning. The bubbly receptionist was nowhere to be found. Last time they were here, she'd buzzed around like a fly on shit, implementing fake meetings through coded words and phrases so the doctor could excuse himself from their conversation. Maro couldn't deny the feeling that something was wrong.

"Should we call for backup?" Ameno said as he reached for his radio.

"Not yet, let's just see what we find first."

Hernandez's warning replayed in Maro's head. *By the books, Ben,* she had said. The fewer people in the room, the easier it was to cover up any questionable tactics. He went behind the desk, looking for anything that stood out, but everything seemed to be in place.

Ameno called out the doctor's name a few times. The forced air spilling through the vents was the only sound.

"Let's check his office," Maro said, already moving toward the closed door. He knocked three times to no response. Jiggling the handle, the detective discovered it was unlocked and quietly pushed it open.

Standing in the doorway, the office appeared normal. Everything tucked in place—except for an expensive man's dress shoe peeking out from behind the desk.

The detectives rushed over to see a body sprawled on the floor. Maro put two fingers to the neck, which was covered in thick red blood, confirming what they already knew. Dr. Daniel DaVadere was dead.

The office was completely intact, indicating there had been no struggle. The stab wound to his neck was small, but effective. Based on the intimacy of the crime scene, Maro could guess the doctor knew his killer. More so, that he'd been caught off guard, leaving no time to defend himself.

"Call it in," Maro said, grudgingly accepting that a stab wound to Dan's neck ended his chance at finding out any additional details from the doctor. His first thought would have been suicide, but the lack of weapon nearby made that theory impossible.

Someone got to the pedophile doc first and the NYPD were going to have a field day. Two Jersey City cops calling in the dead body of an Upper East Side doctor? Any snafu on the case would surely be blamed on "boys across the river not knowing how to handle a big city crime scene." As expected, as soon as the local cops arrived, Maro and Ameno were pushed back behind crime tape. City detectives pulled them to the side, asking what they'd seen and why they'd wanted to talk to that doctor.

Maro understood their names would surely only be mentioned if the case went to shit, but didn't mind the big ol' boys in blue taking the credit. He was focused on his case back in Jersey. Killing someone midday, in a surprise attack, screamed personal, and he could think of a few people who wanted the doctor dead.

CHAPTER 45

Ara paced her living room, picking the dead ends off her hair. Anything to occupy her mind. Lane still hadn't returned her calls. The only thing she hated more than waiting around was not knowing what was happening. Not having control of what was to come, left simply with her own thoughts and morbid imagination. Her phone buzzed, Lane's name flashing across the screen.

Finally. He texted he was on his way up.

She ran to the bathroom and splashed water on her face. Dark shadows hung below her eyes, but there was no time to cover her imperfections with makeup.

Ara ran up to him and tried to grab his hand, but he pulled away, moving past her, sitting instead on the couch. He held his head in his hands, then brushed his hair back, pulling his jaw tight.

"I'm sorry I ignored some of your calls. I've just been thinking a lot since this morning."

Sitting next to him she tried again to touch him, but he flinched, pulling away from her. "I don't know why I didn't tell you the whole story about Dan sooner, and I know that's not good enough, I should have, and I know that, but it's just something I'm not proud of."

"That's what you think this is about?" he asked. "Seriously, Ara, I've been trying so hard to be here for you, but you are making this so difficult." Lane pushed himself off the couch, the words coming out of his mouth barely audible, but no less forceful. "You're no better than him, Ara. Either of them, Brad or Dan. I know you have been through hell, but all you can think about is yourself." His raspy, hushed tone hardly hid the pain in his voice. "I've been here for you, day in and day out. I've held you almost every night for months, lying there until you fall asleep and after all this time, you still feel nothing for me. You still can't tell me you love me, and I just can't take it anymore, Ara."

"What are you saying, Lane, that all I care about is myself?" Tears poured from her eyes, but Ara didn't care what she looked like now. He was seeing her for exactly what she was. "You want to think I'm this perfect little thing who's worth defending, but I'm not. Trust me on this, you don't want to love someone like me."

Lane shook his head, disagreeing. "No, that's where you are wrong. You surround yourself with men who need you damaged. They get off on it even, and you play right into them. I'm not here to defend you, I love you, Ara, but I'm not so sure you love me back, and that's not fair."

"You keep saying that, *I love you,* like it's no big deal. How are you so sure that you love me, maybe you're just getting off on my problems, too, you think of that? You only came into my life after my husband was murdered. Before that you barely noticed me."

"Sure, Ara," he said, laughing. "If that's what you think. That I like getting off on your problems." He stood, walking to the door only to turn back. "Is it so crazy to think that someone could actually love you for you? Despite the endless cycle of nonsense that follows you."

"Well who am I Lane, what do you think you love about me?"

"Everything, since I laid eyes on you at that first New Year's Eve party."

Her words spilled from her mouth before she could stop them. "Even if you talked to me back then, I wouldn't have picked you. Is that the girl you know and love? The girl who would have picked a flashy relationship and security over something real?"

"You're right." Lane looked disrupted. Raw emotion seeped through his appearance, his eyes fighting not to show the tears welling up inside of them. He could only nod, saying, "How could I ever think that you would want to be with me over a cheat and a liar. How could I have been so stupid?" He grabbed her face with both hands and kissed her. Hard, with intention.

Just as quickly, he turned to leave, slamming the door behind him. The wind knocked out of her, Ara fell to her knees, rocking back and forth, trying to catch her breath. Of course, she loved Lane. Why could she never hold on to the good things?

CHAPTER 46

An unremitting tapping on the door convinced her to drag herself from bed. Her first thought was Lane, but he had a key, there was no reason for him to knock. Even Arabelle could let herself in if needed. Glancing at a wall mirror she hardly recognized her face. Dark pockets squished up her eyes until they were almost completely closed, her face spotted with bright pink raised patches of skin. The liquor and God knows how many hours of sweat-filled sleep hung in the surrounding air. In almost a full year of rock bottoms, this one proved to be a new low.

Without even looking through the peephole, Ara swung the heavy door back, only to regret answering instantly. Maro and Ameno stood there, looking taken aback. Ameno even went as far to wave his hand left to right in front of his face.

"Rough night?"

"You could say that. What do you want at this hour?"

"It's after 8 p.m., Ara," Maro said.

"Sure." She paused, trying to put together her day. "You'll have to excuse me, my life these days, it can be a lot," she said sarcastically, leaning into her hip from being unbalanced.

The detectives looked at each other, back to Ara, and then past her, checking for any other people in the apartment.

"Can we come in? You may want to be sitting down for this."

Ara moved to the side and dramatically motioned with her left hand to enter. She walked past them as they seated themselves on the couch and returned moments later with a single glass of water, offering nothing to her guests. Gulping the entire glass after adding an Alka-Seltzer. Arabelle would be so proud.

Ameno cleared his throat, cutting to the chase. "We found Dr. Daniel DaVedere unresponsive in his office yesterday."

Ara nodded blankly, not listening to a word he said.

"He's dead, murdered. Stab wound to the neck."

Dead. Dead. Dead. Ara said the word to herself three times before saying it out loud. "Dead?"

"Yes. He's gone."

Another one, gone.

"We think he knew whoever did it. Surprised him at his desk, bam," Ameno said.

Bam, just like that. Ara cringed at the thought, a life being taken in just one syllable. *Bam*. "That's hard to hear, I'm sorry."

Nodding, Maro said, "Us too. But . . . we have to ask. Given your history with the doctor, and the recent story you shared with us, where were you yesterday morning?"

"Not a story, Detective. *Facts*. Hard facts, as in the truth."

"Yes, damning facts about the doc and how he manipulated you into a sexual relationship. It's just funny, you tell us this, we go to question him and he's dead? Seems a little suspicious."

Ara had to agree. The circumstances certainly seemed convenient. If only she'd kept her mouth shut for a few more hours, her secret would have died with Dan.

"I was home yesterday morning, sleeping."

"Can you think of anyone, a family member, friend . . . Someone who may want to seek some sort of revenge in your honor that would hurt Dr. Daniel DaVedere?"

Everyone in the room knew they were only speaking of one friend. Lane.

"Lane was at work."

Maro pressed his lips, forcing a disapproving silence.

Again, Ara assured, "He was with me, Detective, until his shift that morning."

Realizing neither detective wanted to accept her answer, she stood, showing them the door. "If you have any further questions, you can take them up with Lane or with my attorney." The Alka-Seltzer was boiling in her stomach and up the back of her throat.

Maro stood, but Ameno remained perched on the end of the couch.

"Ara, we want to make sense of this for you. You seem to have a lot of bad circumstances happen around you, and it's our job to figure out why. For you and the other victims." Maro was practically pleading for her to cooperate, tell them anything that could lead somewhere, anywhere.

"No one else knew. I should have never said anything to anyone." Her eyes were wet with tears, a few spilling to her chin as guilt came over her.

Maro placed an arm around her, guiding her back to where she was sitting.

"Between you and me, if what you are saying about your past with him is true, then DaVedere got what he deserved. I'm not supposed to say things like that, but for me, it's the truth. We need you to help us figure it all out. You have to have some idea of who wants to do this to the people around you."

Sobbing into her hands, Ara could feel the stirring in her stomach. She was the connection between Brad and Dan. She knew that. There was nothing else bridging these cases together. Though her relationship with Dan was more than strained, she hated that someone had ended his life. Mood depending, she considered him one of her life's greatest loves, as screwed up as it was.

When Brad died, a part of her left with him. He was ingrained in her like a habit of the worst kind. Oxygen couldn't help her live without him. Dependence does not always equal love. The last time she saw Dan, she nearly gauged his eyeballs out.

"Are you sure Dan didn't kill himself?" she asked, in between her shortening breaths. "He knew what he did and that I could prove it. I had plenty of emails and texts to do so. It would ruin his reputation; he would lose his license. That alone might cause him to kill himself."

Nodding again, Maro said, "Makes sense. But there's no knife. The damn thing couldn't have walked away."

"Stabbing seems personal. Especially if he didn't fight back," she said.

"Yes, that's the theory we're working."

Ameno reached for his cell phone, turning on the voice recorder before Maro waved his hand, signaling to him that this was off the record. Once the phone was back in his pocket, Ara continued.

"Brad and Dan . . . you should learn more about men like them. Their lives, they're not clean. Both of them loved risk." Squinting, Ara tried to remained focused on Ameno. She had already won over his partner. "They used people. Each in their own way. Women were nothing but objects to them. Strong women don't fall for that kind of crap, but they picked ones who yearned to feel pretty and loved. The desperate ones. Myself included."

Shaking his head, Ameno said, "I don't believe you fall into that category. We know you can be strong when you have to be, calculated even. You don't think they loved you?"

Not the way Lane does. Her throat burned, stomach flipped, and seconds later she threw up into her water cup.

CHAPTER 47

Harley gathered the bubbles floating on top of the steaming hot water, forming a lilac-scented mound that resembled an ice cream sundae above her navel. She'd always loved the doctor's bathroom. Especially its large soaking tub. Taking a sip of expensive champagne, she let her head fall back, breathing in the sweet scent of luxury from the foam.

Two years was a long time for someone like her to stick around. But then she met Dan and began dedicating every moment to him, never feeling she could completely pay off the debt she owed. At twenty-three, her world had crashed and burned at her feet. Leaving her homeless, addicted to drugs, and worse, helpless to recover from a childhood dream that failed her. Returning back to her hick hometown in Indiana was a failure she couldn't endure. The ruthless small towners would relish in pitiless "I told you so's," her family especially. So instead, she resorted to the seedy life of many spent models, stripping first before finding her way into a high-end escort service.

It was through the latter that she met Dr. Daniel DaVadere. A

young, attractive doctor, brooding in heartbreak at a well-to-do bar in

the world's most fabulous city. A former flame had officially broken

things off the night before, an ending he didn't see coming, or so he

claimed. He wooed her with fairytales of their romance and found

comfort with her warm, curved body lying next to him. She'd fallen

asleep praying that a man who could love so deeply might one day wake

up and fall in love with her, too. It seemed like a reasonable ask of

whatever higher power existed up there.

The doctor plucked her from wretchedness, giving her a well-

paying position as his executive assistant and making sure she never

wanted for anything again—not a new dress or an orgasm. He treated

her for free, helping her to overcome her addictions and past. Despite a

passion-filled affair, he could never be exclusive to her, nor did he

promise that. He respected Harley, never parading another woman in

front of her, but it was made clear she needed to accept the terms of their

open circumstance. And accept she did.

It wasn't until his mood began to deteriorate that she first

snooped. Learning quickly of his obsession with his past and the secret pay as you go phone he kept hidden in his top right desk drawer. The distance grew between them, and he barely spoke to her let alone touched her in recent days. And if he did, it was only to spin her around, bend her over his desk, and take her from behind. Smashing into her, hard and angry.

It was no different today. If he'd at least looked up at her when she walked into his office, killing him would not have been so easy. But he didn't even look at her, too entranced by his own worries to notice her lip quivering. But nervousness aside, she knew she needed to free Dan from his unhealthy obsession and free herself of hers.

He'd angrily brushed away her hand when she'd touched his shoulder. Retreating, she'd taken a step back, then switched the knife behind her back from her left hand to right and tightened her grip. She'd asked around some of her old hangouts if anyone knew where she could get a gun. These were working women, not fools. They certainly weren't about to help the old competition blow a bullet through one of her Johns. So, she'd gone with a knife.

She'd exhaled. Loudly. A final warning that he should acknowledge her existence but even that went unnoticed.

Look up. See me, she had silently begged before forcing the knife with both hands into his neck. *All you had to do was look at me.* He'd fallen, slumped down to the floor with his eyes still forward, never giving her the satisfaction.

She'd feared she wouldn't have enough strength to drive the knife into his neck. That he would overtake her, slit her throat instead. Oddly, it wasn't very hard at all.

Expecting to feel a horrible sense of guilt and not wanting to leave behind her DNA, she'd satirically blew a kiss in his direction and wrapped herself in her mid-length trench coat, tucking the knife into the coat's deep pockets. Leaving the office just as it was, minus the life she had taken.

Now, here in the tub, Dan's blood already showered away, she held the knife. A simple tool, imbued with so much purpose. A knife they had once used to chop vegetables while making a stir fry together over one of Dan's favorite Napa cabs. Happy memories tied to a desperate, sickening finale. Slowly, she dragged the sharp edge over her forearm, a bright red stripe of blood trailing behind the blade. Now they each bled by the same means and that connection brought her a sense of fulfillment.

Her blood trickled into the steaming pool, its red color dissipating into the clear water, leaving behind no sign the two had ever mixed.

Finishing her champagne, she reached for Dan's phone, scrolling between the only two contacts. She waited for hours to finally complete her plan.

Come meet me. My place.

She watched as the phone marked the text message as read. She waited patiently, staring at the three teasing dots until the response flashed across the screen.

Why should I?

Someone was playing hard to get.

Because I need you. Now. She knew Dan well enough to mimic his tone.

Moments later the response buzzed across the screen. *On my way.*

That was also easier than she'd expected.

316

She was just going to confront her, not even attempt to hurt her. She just wanted to know how she kept him, what control she had over him. *Maybe it's scotch-flavored nipples,* she thought, laughing at the absurdity of such a thing. Harley had given him everything. A petite frame, perfect cup-sized breasts, and an open, unquestioning love. They would cheer on New York's sports teams and experiment with fine wines and delicately-created dishes at its finest restaurants. Dan finally seemed to be crossing the commitment threshold when something, or someone, blasted him back to his past, tearing him from her arms. Closing him off to her forever. Whoever this woman was, Harley had to meet her.

CHAPTER 48

Raina wanted to vomit. She couldn't look at her own reflection without gagging.

Raina's conscience was always forgiving. While Ara and other girlfriends lamented their growing number of sexual partners or hemmed and hawed over skipping out on plans, Raina could remove all regret from her mind. Not everyone could win in life, and she easily made the relentless moves that caused others to fill up with guilt. But tonight, the city streets seemed darker, stained with an impending sense of doom, and her guilt wouldn't stay locked up. She was only a block or so away when the doctor texted her, so she finished off another martini, not wanting to seem too desperate. The doorman recognized her and nodded as she passed through the entranceway and into the gold-plated elevator doors.

The relationship between her and the doctor had lost its luster quickly.

She shouldn't have expected more from him. They'd literally bumped into each other on a New York street. Outside of romantic comedies and daytime soaps, random situations like that rarely led to long-term happiness. Raina didn't mind; he was good in bed and drank expensive wine. In her world, that made for an above-average hook up.

The doors sprang open, revealing the brightly-lit corridor. To the left of each apartment flickered a bronze lantern-style fixture, giving the long hall an extra touch of elegance. One could judge the wealth in a building by its corridors, Raina always thought. Obviously, the electric bill was not a topic on this building's board meeting agenda.

Her cell phone buzzed in her purse, startling her. Arabelle's name flashed across the screen. Lately the only reason she called was Ara, the last person that Raina wanted to think about right now.

Raina knocked quietly, then moved the door handle. She could tell the door was unlocked, so she showed herself in.

Other than the classic rock that purred quietly from the doctor's bluetooth speaker, the apartment was still. Raina briefly glanced in each of the rooms, calling Dan's name. He couldn't be too far or else the speaker would lose its connection to his phone. Back in the bedroom, light splintered from the crack of the bathroom door, and she could hear water running.

Raina removed her coat and adjusted her breasts until her cleavage sat full and plump in the center of her plunging neckline. Opting to leave her high heels on, she got comfortable on the bed, propping herself up onto her right side, brushing her hair over one shoulder.

Moments later, the water clicked off and the door opened.

"What the hell?" Raina yelled, sitting up on the bed as a young woman exited the bathroom, tightening the doctor's bathrobe around her. "Who are you?"

"I'm Harley, Dr. DaVedere's executive assistant."

Raina lowered her doubtful stare, focusing on Harley's lack of clothing and obvious level of comfort in the doctor's apartment.

"What does he want, a three-way or something?" Raina swung her legs to stand up from the bed. "He could have told me that before I came over." She walked to a corner table with a crystal scotch decanter sitting in the middle and gave herself a large pour before taking it down like a shooter. *That was one thing about the doctor, you could always find a drink in every room of his apartment.* "I'm not totally against it, just like to know in advance if I'm going to have to bend that way, you know?"

"That's not why I called you here tonight," Harley said. "I called you because I wanted to see you in person. See what you had, what it was about you that enamored him so."

"Excuse me? I'm not sure who you're talking about, but I can sure as hell tell you he didn't think of me that way." Raina poured herself a second drink.

"I needed to see why he picked you over me. He was like a little school boy. Obsessed and love sick. Desperately devoted, until I stabbed him, of course. I needed to get you here to see you in person. See what he loved about you over me."

Raina's internal antenna quivered, a sudden sense of danger quickening her pulse. She bolted toward her cell phone, the glass she was holding falling to the floor. Harley rushed toward her as she fumbled with the phone, stripping it from Raina's hand and pushing her back up against the wall. The phone ricocheted across the room.

Holding Raina, Harley said through her teeth, "I just want to talk. I just need to know. Please."

Raina pushed back against Harley's shoulders and blindly pulled down on her hair, sending Harley flailing into an awkward arched position. Raina cracked her in the face with her fist, then shifted sideways, still gripping a handful of hair. She reached for a decorative iron sconce on the nightstand. Harley tried to swing out from under Raina's arm to break loose but was no match due to the incapacitating position.

"Don't do this, Ara, please!" Harley yelled.

Before Raina could even register that name, she swung the solid sconce, meeting Harley's skull with a disorienting crack and sending a splatter of red across Dan's ivory bedding. With Harley now on the floor, knocked unconscious by the hit, she grabbed her phone off the floor and started to dial 911 before deciding against it.

Raina let out a scream dropping the decorative piece, still in her right hand, to the ground. *What exactly just happened, and how did it escalate so quickly? What did Ara have to do with the doctor? Had she heard this clearly sick, sick woman correctly? Or was she really losing her mind?*

Kneeling beside the crumpled woman, Raina reached into the bathrobe's pocket, looking for any indication of who this woman was. Finding another cell phone, she quickly accessed the phone's recent messages, horrified to see that the only two saved phone numbers were both under a single letter named contact.

Had the woman, now unconscious on the floor, just been trying to warn her? How was everyone in New York entwined with Ara?

If there was ever a time Raina wished she had not been drinking, it was now. With more questions than answers, there was only one thing that seemed crystal clear. She desperately needed to speak with Ara. Tossing the phone to the ground, she bolted from the apartment.

CHAPTER 49

Ameno and Maro weaved through the West Side Highway's evening traffic, turning the undercover car's flashers on when needed.

The doctor had creeped Maro out from the get-go. He couldn't fathom a situation where he would spend money to send a teenage daughter for quality time with that quack; then again, he couldn't fathom much about raising a teenage daughter. But now the quack wasn't just some overpriced perv looking to get his dick touched by young girls—he was a murder victim, and under Maro's professional code that meant he had to think of him as a vic, not a criminal.

Maro shook his head. "Can't be a coincidence. Two guys involved with the same woman, ending up dead? There's gotta be a connection there." Maro whizzed past a town car moving too slow for the left lane. "Doesn't mean Ara did it. Someone in her circle though . . ."

"Think we're working with the whole line-up? Someone could have gotten called up to handle the job." Maro hated when Ameno used sports references to refer to real life situations; they weren't picking their starters for a fantasy football team off a bench here. They were trying to solve a murder case.

"Not sure." One day he'd get his kid partner to realize less is often more. And silence was freakin' golden. Maro pulled back into the right lane and clicked on his turn signal.

"Where we headed?"

Maro seesawed between considering his partner was super naive or just a dumbass. "By the doc's apartment."

"But it's not our case."

Do I have to spell everything out for you? "Maybe not, but he was the suspect in *our* case. There may be something there, and we need to find out about it before it gets locked away in a box with NYPD."

The building's security guard didn't take much convincing and escorted them to the doctor's front door. They found it wide open, providing more than enough probable cause to enter. Ameno nodded to the guard, who stayed behind them. Maro and Ameno raised their guns as they cleared the front rooms and kitchen.

When they reached the bedroom, the guard jumped back at the sight of a woman's bludgeoned body.

"Looks like we found our assistant," Maro said. Harley laid bloody on the floor. He never got used to finding a body. It repulsed him when a life, whether promising or not, was snuffed out too soon. Not at the hands of God, but self-serving counterfeits playing the role. Unlike the scene at the office, signs of a struggle were strewn across the bedroom. Her eyes, suddenly opened wide, showed the kind of fear one could only feel when fearing their life was going to end. Maro kneeled down and pressed his hand to her neck. "She's alive!"

Ameno yelled out to the guard to call 911 before kneeling next to the victim. Harley, coming to, nervously shifted her stare between the detectives.

"My name is Detective Maro and this is my partner Detective Ameno. We are here to help you. We've met before, remember, at Dr. Dan's office." He took out a handkerchief from his pocket and placed it over her gaping head wound. "Do you remember what happened here, who attacked you?"

Before Harley could answer, the guard rushed back in the room. "Cops are on their way." After a disapproving look from Maro, he corrected, "You know, NYPD."

326

If not for the injured woman at his feet, Maro would have physically removed him from the scene. Ameno, for once picking up on his signals, stood to force the guard out and search the rest of the apartment before others arrived to the scene.

"We got a knife in here. Next to the tub," he called from the bathroom. "Tub's full."

At the mention of the knife, Harley broke down, "I'm so sorry," she wailed, bringing both hands up to cover her face.

"Calm down, you're going to be OK."

"No I won't, I will never be OK because of her. I didn't want to do it, but I had to." She sobbed, beginning to become hysterical.

Maro gestured toward Ameno to look down, laying in the center of the room was a pay-as-you-go smartphone. Ameno took two latex gloves from his pocket and pulled them on. He scrolled through the messages, with only two contacts, one listed as A and one R. Clicking out of the recent conversations he pressed the photo icon. A phone's photo often held valuable evidence, sometimes in the happy moments captured before a tragic event, where the owner clearly didn't know what was coming, and others in a brave effort to expose an attacker for what they were.

This photo stream revealed something even stranger. First there were seductive photos of Raina, but if you scrolled further into the stream there were hundreds of photos of Ara Hopkins dating back months, years maybe. Images of her both alone and with others, with Brad and more recently her with Lane.

"You gotta be shitting me," Ameno said, scrolling further and further back in time.

Maro stood, excited by what Ameno had found.

"Is that Ara?"

"You betcha. Ara, Raina, Lane. Brad. The gang's all here in high res."

"Jesus Christ. Is this the doc's phone?" It certainly looked like it.

Turning his attention back to Harley, who was now struggling to sit up against the bed, he said, "Do you know whose phone this is?" He rolled latex gloves onto his hands and snatched the phone from his partner.

"Of course I do. It's his, Dr. Dan's. I took it with me from the office after I killed him." Her candor caught him off guard.

"You killed the doctor?"

"Yes, then I took the phone and asked her to meet me here. I just wanted to meet her. See her face to face. But she freaked out and attacked me."

Maro frantically scrolled through the stream, finding a picture of Ara, then held it out in front of Harley's face, "Is this her, the girl you wanted to meet?"

On cue, paramedics and two NYPD officers entered the apartment with the security guard, rushing over to Harley. Maro, placing one hand up for them to pause repeated his question, "Is this the girl that did this to you?"

Harley defeated, shook her head back and forth. "No."

Rattled that the doctor's receptionist did not recognize Ara, he scrolled back through the photos, wondering who else could have done this to Harley.

"That's enough, Detective, she's injured," the New York officer said.

Stopping on one of the more recent photos, Raina Martin posing seductively in front of a mirror, he turned the phone back toward Harley. "Just one more. Is this who attacked you?"

Dissolving into tears, Harley shook her head yes.

Standing back, his mind rushed with the evidence now in front of him.

Going back in the photo stream until last February, there, right in front of him, were photos of Brad Bugia's last night alive. He searched each image before moving on to the next. The final thumbnail from that night was not a photo, but a video of what looked like the street in front of Brad and Ara's apartment building.

"Well, what do we have here?" he said, pressing the play button. The scene unraveled in front of him. Ara getting out of the Uber, pausing on the street corner, taking a few moments before entering through the doors, disappearing into the black space of time they had desperately been trying to fill. The video, still recording, flip flopped to face downwards as the person filming fumbled around the car. Seconds later, the camera was jarred back up, focusing on the door.

"Shit." Maro dragged the video back, replaying it for Ameno. "Get Bene on the phone."

The two detectives looked at each other, eyes wide. "We've been going after the wrong sister."

CHAPTER 50

Lane, sitting in his squad car, tried to process what he just heard. Ara's doctor had been following her almost nightly to work events and social outings both before and after Brad's death, even capturing intimate moments he had thought were shared between just him and her? NYPD was in the process of tearing through years of files at the doc's uptown office, while a separate crew processed the assault that had taken place in the doctor's bedroom on his executive assistant and lover, Harley Petit.

The catch? It was not an attempted murder-suicide. Couldn't have been. Each were targets in what seemed to be separate, surprise attacks. The even bigger surprise, photos of Raina were found on the doctor's pay as you go phone.

"We need you to get in contact with Ms. Hopkins and bring her down to the station. She may be in danger, Bene," Maro told him.

A sudden wave of guilt crushed his chest. He had left her all alone, abandoned her over something insignificant, and now she could be in trouble. How could he have been so selfish?

Maro continued, "There's evidence on the phone, but we can talk more later. I can't have another victim here, and she wasn't in the best shape when we left her. Ara trusts you. Please. Get her to meet us at the station in Jersey, we can explain later."

"What do you mean? What kind of shape was she in when you left her? When did you see Ara last?" The heaviness on Lane's chest intensified into a violent panic.

Ameno came on the line. "Just get your girl, Bene. We'll meet you at the station."

"Dammit!" Lane slammed both hands against the dashboard. Nervously tapping the steering wheel, he flipped on his squad car lights and raced through the intersection. His rear right side barely escaped a blow by an oncoming mini-van that screeched to a halt in the road's shoulder.

No matter how he dissected the brief conversation with the New Jersey detectives, Lane couldn't figure out what he was about to walk into. All he did know was that Ameno and Maro were concerned for Ara, for once. Of course, there was the possibility that they were pulling a fast one, having him hand deliver her for an arrest on a silver platter, but he pushed that thought from his mind, hoping they finally had the

evidence to eliminate her as a suspect.

A toxic combination of rage and fear was brewing. He needed to

get to Ara, and fast.

CHAPTER 51

When push came to shove, people always chose themselves.

Despite their obvious differences, Raina and Ara had always balanced one another, Raina's booming personality compensated for Ara's understated demeanor. Together at college, the pair demanded the attention from every room they entered, resulting in full social calendars and the hottest hook ups, followed up with fast food splurges and Laguna Beach marathons. At that time, it was enough to concoct the perfect relationship for two girls forced together by their parents.

As they grew into women, the bond solidified to a dependence allowing Ara to let her guard down. Making her foolish enough to think their bond was unbreakable. She should have known Raina would always choose Raina first.

The first time Ara heard the voicemail, it stopped her dead in her tracks. Sucked the air out of her so fast that she nearly collapsed right then and there. But it was amazing what you could make yourself immune to if you forced yourself to endure it. Over and over and over, for a year. Now, she could practically recite it word for word.

She says she loves you. But does she show it? I love you, Brad

Bugia, and will show you that every day of your life. I won't go on how

we are now, especially now that you know she's pregnant. Do you want

to be stuck in a family with her? We both know we didn't mean for this

to happen between you and me, but it did, and you are everything to me

now. Please be smart, think about what you want and who you want in

your future, not just the next few days but forever. You're bored with

her; I promise you a lifetime of adventure. Free yourself. I love you.

Follow the plan and do the right thing.

As she'd walked up the cold stairs of her apartment building that

night, Ara lost a little more confidence with every step she took, leaving

her hesitant and unstable by the time she reached the top. At the start of

the hike up, she'd known exactly what she needed to do. But step by

step, she'd left a tiny piece of certainty on each landing.

Reaching into her clutch, Ara had pulled out her cell phone,

clicking into her voice recordings. She had felt so guilty the day she

recorded it. It was after a decent session between the sheets, when Brad

was showering, that Ara's world was destroyed. The name, flashing brightly across his phone's screen, taunted her with its cruelty. It was a rare occasion that Brad's phone was not tucked in his pocket or pushed off somewhere out of her sight. It was only after she decided to snoop that she realized how inaccessible it really was, practically glued to him at all times. He'd answer or ignore calls swiftly, swiping away call and text alerts like a grand pianist. Shrouding his life, and his lies, with short easy actions.

Not that night. *Ding.* Voicemail. It was 2 a.m. on Friday night. Even work colleagues resorted to email or text at this hour. With only a few tries, Ara gained access into the phone. Why had she never tried to guess his password before?

Then she heard it. The voice on the other end, belligerent and forceful with its message. *Now or never.*

At first, devastating pain had consumed her, freezing her from the inside out. But she'd developed an immunity to its viral message after listening to it again and again. No matter how many times she replayed the voicemail, though, Ara still couldn't hold back her tears.

They forced you to do this, she'd told herself as she tucked the phone back in her clutch.

They both deserve this.

CHAPTER 52

Raina sat, feeling numb to the typical subway absurdities. The couple next to her, each not a day over twenty-one, painting pictures of their future together, inches from each other's faces. A future filled with flowery descriptions of social gatherings and climbing the corporate ladder. Only once they reached the top would there be children that they would send off to exclusive private schools where their heads would be filled with the same dreamy nonsense these two were spewing to each other on the train. On a different day, Raina would have told them that it doesn't work out like that; life sucks you in and then beats you down with the relentless fist of reality.

She was too tired today and was still trying to piece together what happened at the doctor's apartment. Staring straight ahead, she barely noticed the hot thirtysomething man asking if she needed help.

"You're as pale as a ghost," he said, sounding genuinely concerned.

More like being haunted by one or two. She smiled and looked down at her phone, the universal sign of "not interested." As the subway pulled into the station, she made her way to the sliding doors and started toward the exit.

"I wasn't just hitting on you, you know." The concerned passenger jogged up to meet her.

"It sure seems like it," she said, keeping her glance forward.

"Do you need me to call someone for you? You look like you might pass out."

This guy doesn't quit.

"Listen, normally I would be super into this attention, and I'd bat my eyes, play damsel in distress. We'd end up at a bar and after a few dirty martinis, I'd be riding you raw. Confirming for you that you really are *a great guy*. But I don't have time for this today, and I need you to leave me the hell alone."

She stormed past him, tempted to turn around, reel the poor bastard back in and escape to his place. A random man's apartment sounded like the best place to hide from the police. Any moment they would find something that pointed directly to her in the doctor's apartment. She was sure of it. The detectives would connect the dots, moments later hauling her away for the murder of some random bitch.

340

Did she actually kill that woman? If she did, it was an accident, but still, how could she be so stupid? Of all the things she'd done in her life, this was going to be the thing that brought her down.

Ara had to be the mastermind behind Raina's current unfortunate situation. What did she know, and what was her plan, setting her up like this? But there were too many holes in that theory. In less than ten minutes, she would be at Ara's apartment, demanding answers.

We need to talk. On my way. She typed into her phone. The three small dots showing Ara's unsent response taunted her all the way to her apartment.

A nagging thought wouldn't leave Raina's mind. Somehow deep down she knew, only one of them was going to make it out of this unscathed.

Ara answered the door just a few seconds after Raina knocked. Clearly waiting for her arrival. Without saying a word, she moved to the side, indicating for her to come in, eyeing Raina as she walked through the door and into the living room.

Ara's lips gathered into a stressed crease, pulling the skin tight on her face and revealing sunken cheeks and large, shaded bags under her eyes. Raina knew she had been crying. She'd watched Ara's heart break

enough times.

It was a rare occasion that neither of them knew what to say. The

ugly road they were about to start down was so dark, but after years of

what on the surface seemed to be a healthy, supportive sistership, they

had reached their final destination.

"What do you know?" Raina demanded, tucking loose strands of

hair behind her ears, trying not to show how uncomfortable she was.

But Ara wasn't going to let her lead the conversation, she made

that clear. "I don't know what you're talking about. I *know* a lot of

things."

"Tell me, Ara. Tell me everything. I'm not going to play your

manipulative games tonight."

"*My* games?" Ara's voice rose well above the volume of a

normal conversation, "You have some nerve, Raina Martin, do you

know that? You sleep with my husband while pretending to be a sister to

me, then you decide you don't have time for 'games'?"

Raina flinched. Not that Ara's anger wasn't uncalled for after

finding out her husband was having an affair with her stepsister, but it was uncommon, unnatural even, coming from Ara. Her backbone must have aligned. *Damn you, Brad, why did you leave me alone in this mess?* Raina thought.

"We didn't want it to happen, Ara. But it did. We couldn't help it!"

Ara exploded in a scary fit of laughter. "Don't kid yourself, Raina. You totally wanted it to happen. You wanted to be able to hurt me anyway you could. You're a no good whore and that's all you ever were to him. Not someone he could be proud of. A dirty little secret he wouldn't even brag to his single friends about in a locker room."

"You have no idea what he felt for me!" Raina trembled at the thought of Brad being embarrassed of her. She'd loved him. It wasn't her fault the universe had played a sick joke, allowing them both to fall in love with the same man.

Ara's eyes pierced through Raina's skin. Focused and fierce, and for the first time Raina was afraid of her. The hatred burning through her eyes could only manifest from her knowing everything.

"You told me once you'd never hate me, that we were sisters," Raina said.

"Sisters don't do what you did, and you know that."

Shaking her head vigorously, left to right, Raina said, "You're wrong there, Ara. We always hurt the people we love the most."

"That's your excuse for sleeping with my husband, destroying my life? You did all of that to me because you just love me so much? You wanted him to kill me, Raina, am I supposed to just move past that?"

"Ara," Raina begged.

"I regret everything. Meeting you, taking care of you. Being your friend and standing beside you as your sister. God, like that wasn't a job in itself! Allowing you in my life was one of the worst decisions I have ever made. Hate doesn't even begin to describe what I feel for you. I loathe you!"

The words stung more than she expected. Without even realizing what she was doing, she reached into her bag, grabbed hold of the cold metal inside, and aimed a handgun at her stepsister.

CHAPTER 53

Ara tried to remain calm, yet with death taunting her at the hands

of someone she once trusted, she questioned whether any of it was worth

it. Brad, Raina, her New York glitz and glam life. Somewhere deep

down inside of her, she had to know the game she was getting into with

Brad. She had to know that men like that didn't love only you forever. If

they could ever stop loving themselves long enough to love you at all.

What she would do right now to disappear into a small town in the

middle of the country. Give it all up, work at a coffee shop. *Baristas*

must live the best lives. Was that really going to be her final thought?

She would come home, make small talk about her day with Lane before

they'd tumble into the bedroom. Or onto the kitchen floor.

Lane. Why couldn't the universe just have given him to her first?

His recent confession that he loved her since that first New Year's Eve

party so many years ago . . . That night, like many of her nights, started

with her being irritated with Raina and ended with Brad sweeping her

off her feet. Forcing her into a daze she was just breaking free from in

this very moment. Funny how life brought you right back to where you started, despite all your efforts to move straight forward away from the messes you encounter along the way.

If only Brad knew that night, his last night, how their life together would end. The moment was still clear in her head. It was one she would never forget. She had paused to take one more breath to fill her lungs before opening the door to their perfect apartment. Brad was sitting wide legged on their sofa, an elbow on each upper thigh and head in hands. The tiniest inkling of sweat outlining his hairline, despite the freezing temperatures outside. Clearly deep in his own thoughts, he hadn't noticed her until she closed the door behind her, louder than normal on purpose.

Startled, he'd looked up at her. She could see in his eyes, for just a moment, a cloud of sadness. For a man who identified himself as always being able to manipulate a situation, he'd for once lost hold of the reins. That night he was torn between what to do and what he had promised.

"We need to talk."

"I know." He would never see her cry over this.

346

"Things have changed so much the past few years. And you and I, we've changed also. I didn't see it happening at first." He brushed his hair back with both hands dramatically, a slight tremor popping his heel from the floor. "And then it was like BAM! Right in my face."

Ara flinched, hanging on every word of his explanation. Desperate to see him at work, justifying what he was about to do to her. As if it could be justified.

"I never wanted to hurt you, Ara. You're just too . . ." He stood, shifting his weight as he considered his next words carefully. "It just wasn't as easy as it first seemed when we met."

"Is that what you wanted? Someone who was easy?" Like a movie playing in her head, she saw him offering Raina the slightest attention, just a few strokes to her ego to get her grinding like a porn star. His head tilted back, enjoying every second of pleasure he didn't need to work for. Was that really all it took for him to throw his life with her away?

"Buffets are easy, Brad, but it certainly doesn't mean the food's good." It felt like a horrible clichéd statement when she said it, but somehow it fit to her horribly clichéd life.

She let him walk up to touch her, side stepping at the last
moment into position. His back now to the door, just as she had planned.
If only her life plan worked as smoothly.

"But they fill you up, Ara. And sometimes being full is more
important than how it tastes."

Repulsed at his willingness to lower his standards, she didn't
have time to feel sick. Her husband, who only wore custom-tailored
suits, who thrived in a façade of success and perfection, was willing to
throw it all away for easy sex.

In an honest moment, her eyes met his and she wanted to throw
herself at him. Promise she could be easy, too, that everything could be
how he wants it, if only he stopped now. Apologize for anytime she'd let
him down with her moods, or for the times she'd preferred sleep over
sex. Instead, swallowing hard, she reminded herself that despite it all,
her flaws and liabilities, she was worth it. A mantra she had been
repeating to herself all night. After all, it was she who was slumming for
a lying cheat who was plotting to kill her. She deserved better.

"I'm sorry, Ara." The dream that haunted her sleep since she
first heard that voicemail came into her mind. Brad making love to her.

348

Him brushing the hair from her face and kissing her cheek before placing two hands around her neck. Closing off the air supplying life to her body, sending her thrashing for him to release. He'd look down as if she was a problem being solved, before her eyes would roll back, a lonely blackness consuming her.

This wasn't a dream. This was a nightmare, and it was as real as could be. Her husband, who promised to love and cherish her, formed a plan with her stepsister to eliminate her. He went to take a step toward her. She had to stop him before he got any closer, she could not let him gain another inch on her.

"I'm pregnant. I just wanted you to know that before you tried to kill me. I wanted you to know you'd be killing both of us for her."

Slapped with surprise, he had stopped, dead in his step, having no idea she knew his plan. "I know, Ara, I saw the test in the trash and then at dinner tonight, you didn't drink your wine. That's when I knew for sure."

"And you're still going to go through with it?"

Eyes tightly squeezed shut, Ara snapped back to present day, a scene that was eerily similar.

"What is going on here?" Lane stood in the doorway, right hand on his gun, left on his radio, focused on the gun Raina had dropped down to her side.

"What do you think you're doing, Raina?!" he yelled, standing in front of Ara. "God, you crazy, crazy woman. For Chrissake, put the gun down!"

"You don't know anything," she yelled, a mixture of snot and spit escaping her mouth with her words.

"I certainly don't know how you got a gun, that's for damn sure."

What did it matter? Ara thought, her step-sister had one, and she wanted to finish what Brad hadn't.

"Ask her, Lane. Ask her what she did," Raina demanded. Pointing the gun in their direction.

Ara, two palms against Lane's back, inhaled his scent, holding onto its smell in case it was the last time he let her in this close. Just in case he never wanted to speak to her again after knowing what she did.

"Ask her!" Raina yelled pointing the gun more directly behind Lane.

"You need to put the gun down."

"She's a murderer!" Raina yelled as Ara pulled away from Lane, lunging toward her, only to be pulled back. If only he had been there when she murdered Brad to stop her as he just had.

Only she and Brad would ever really know how that night played out.

That night she pulled their gun from her clutch and held it, firmly pointed at his chest. The same gun he had purchased to end her life. The gun that was part of his perfectly-constructed stories of enraged political opponents and Ara's returning depression. "Babe, whoa! Let's talk about it. You don't want to do this," Brad had cried. Desperate for the first time in his life, realizing it could all end so quickly.

Ara had held the gun in her gloved hand, cool. Calm. "No, I don't. But it's me or you, isn't it? That's your great surprise for me tonight. That's why we have this stupid gun."

"You don't know what you're talking about, you're acting crazy," he said.

"I'm the crazy one? You think I don't know what you've been doing behind my back, setting everything up so you could get away with it!" She swallowed the lump making a home in the back of her throat. "I also know that she wants this gun pointed at me, and that you're so whipped, or just plain weak, that you were going to do it. Kill me and your child." She paused. "Your wife. Who you promised to love and protect for the rest of your life."

Hesitantly he moved one foot forward, arms in the air like a common criminal.

"What? I could have never done that." His eyes met hers. "She's the crazy one. Not me. Certainly not you, baby. I didn't mean to say that; this is just getting out of hand."

"You really think I'm so damn stupid!" she'd yelled. "You think so little of me, but you're wrong. I know everything."

Brad took a few more steps toward hers, his arms reaching for her. "I always loved you, Ara. I wasn't going to go through with it. Never."

The last words she heard him say, "I promise," with the same inauthenticity he promised many times before.

She shot him with her eyes squeezed shut, the bullet drilling into the center of his chest. The first time they met was the last thing she saw flash before her eyes. His confident smirk, looking down at her. One night, one look, that sent them spiraling to a doomed conclusion. She had pulled the trigger, eyes tightly closed, and heard his life end on their immaculately polished floor.

The infinite pain of that night returned as she told Lane, sharing each and every detail. Wanting nothing more than to finally come clean.

The last thing Ara wanted was for Lane to look at her the way he was now: confused and overcome with anger. Biting her lip, she shook her head, silently begging him to love her, to understand why she'd had to do the things she did that night.

I never meant to hurt you, Ara. Brad's words stung like a wasp determined to ruin a perfect picnic. He tried to destroy her life, the aftershocks still causing her pain in his death. Standing here in front of Lane, she sadly understood what he'd meant by those five words. Lane was never supposed to be a victim in her revenge. Prior to Brad's death, she hadn't thought much about the consequences of her actions, she didn't plan on having anything to live for. But now, all she wanted was for Lane to see her the way he had moments ago. Falling in love with him was something she hadn't planned for.

"I'm sorry, Lane, please understand." She reached for him, ignoring the gun firmly gripped in his right hand. Holding his hands in hers, she tried to explain.

"Save it, Ara," Raina interrupted. "He's a goddamn cop. He will arrest you. You're nothing but a murderer." Despite Raina's taunting words ringing loud into the room, Lane and her eyes remained locked. The rage was building inside her. Looking up at him, she looked for any sign of understanding. Anything from him at all. But he stood, emotionless before conceding.

"She's right. I'm going to have to call this in, Ara," he said through gritted teeth, eyes stung red at their corners.

"I can explain. It was them, Lane, all them, don't you understand? It would have been me on the floor dead. Brad was going to kill me." She held both of his hands in hers, his right still firm to his gun. Squeezing tighter, she mouthed *I love you,* unable to say them through her tears.

"Boo friggin' hoo. What a love story," Raina yelled through laughter. "You just can't get it right, can you?"

"Shut up," Ara said, her eyes never leaving Lane's.

"It's over, Ara. Brad's laughing at you right now from the grave, I'm sure of it. To think I thought we were going to have to get rid of you! You destroyed yourself."

With one last plea to Lane, hoping one day he could love her again, Ara pulled the gun from his hands, easier than expected. Had he let her? She spun around, directing it straight at Raina. "I said, shut up! How dare you speak to me like that, with what you two were planning? Tell him, Raina, tell him what you demanded Brad do to me."

Lane was speaking fast on Ara's right, trying to be the voice of reason in her head, promising he would always love her, that she didn't need to ruin her life this way. But Ara kept the gun pointed directly on her stepsister, trying her best to tune out Lane's desperate pleas.

"You wouldn't kill me," Raina said.

"Funny, Brad said the same thing." Ara spit.

"OK, fine! I hate you, Ara. I hate everything about you. All prissy and damaged. So many times I wanted to slap you, tell you to grow the hell up. I couldn't stand you got the perfect little life that should have been mine all along."

"You introduced us! How can you be so warped as to convince yourself I took anything from you?"

"Please, I never thought he'd actually go for you, let alone marry you. But no. You and your doe eyes practically moved him right out to the suburbs. But he *was* bored. Miserable. Banging anything that opened its legs at the office. And I realized I could get it all back on track. It could be Brad and me."

It was agonizing hearing the words spewing from her mouth.

"I would have won, too. He was going to kill you. Make it look like a robbery gone wrong, suicide. Whatever he wanted. He established your mental issues just in case. Every time he encouraged you to tackle your demons, he just wanted to lock you up so he could build a story of your insanity. He had no problems at the office, it was all a lie so he could convince you to legally get that gun. You should be dead, not Brad, you!"

Lane now had one hand on Ara's back, the other on her extended arm, inching toward the gun.

"How did you convince him to do it, Raina? That's all I want to know. What did you do to convince my husband he couldn't just divorce me but had to kill me?"

Raina shrieked in amusement. "That's the best part," she said through riled breaths.

"How?" Ara demanded.

Raina laughing harder, shrinking Ara down to feel shamefully small. "I told him I was pregnant. Just. Like. You. And that he had to choose or I would expose everything. It was easier than you would think, Brad was so afraid of what his big congressman daddy would think if he knew about all the affairs and the love child. He had to pick, and he picked me!"

Like a sucker-punch to the face, Ara's body convulsed at the thought. The sound of the shot ricocheted off the walls sending her ears ringing. Lane, just centimeters away from stopping her, wrapped his arms around Ara's waist, falling to his knees, sobbing into the side of her thigh.

A gaping hole in her neck, Raina gurgled something incomprehensible before falling to the floor, her life ending in the same room as Brad's, in some odd sense of irony.

Ara waited for tears, waited to crumble under the brutality of what she'd just done, but she was still as a statue. *Was it worth it?* In her heart, she knew it was. She would never regret what she did. Brad and Raina had left her no other choice, and nothing would force her to feel remorse for choosing herself.

She could feel Lane's embrace slipping down her body. Shaking the picture from her head, she turned and kneeled, moving her eyes in front of his, demanding his attention.

Stern and unshaken, she finally said, "He was going to kill me, you see that now right?"

Trembling, he shook his head back and forth. Taking his gun from her hands, Lane looked back at her horrified. He really saw her now, and she wasn't perfect. She was twice a murderer.

Ara couldn't stand the pained look in his eyes. She wanted to hold him, promise she was the good he believed in. But he looked like he might kill her himself.

"They wanted me dead, please, baby. Listen to what I'm saying. You heard what she said, I would be dead." There was nothing in his eyes that showed agreement. Overcome, she gagged on her tears, sobbing as she placed her forehead to the floor.

With a brush of a kiss to the back of her head, he stood. Untucking the lower part of his shirt, he wiped the grip of the gun before securing it in his own hands and raising it in the direction of Raina's fallen body. Looking up at him, there was nothing more to say.

Ara understood knowing she killed his lifelong friend bore a deep burden, but it was a necessary evil to righting the wrong. Ara had peeled back the ugly layers exposing Brad for exactly who he was. A man who would kill his pregnant wife to save his reputation.

As a genuine, good man, the law taught Lane to believe that murder was never a just solution to a problem. That no crime went unpunished. But she hoped he could see that what she did was simply self-defense flavored with a spit of revenge.

Finally, he said, "I promised you, no matter what, and I meant it."

A hand on her back, Lane guided her toward the door, but she stopped, placing her hands to his cheeks and kissing him, unapologetically. Feeling the quaking behind his lips, she pulled him in, holding him tighter. "I love you, Lane Bene."

Moving back, he nodded and wiped his eyes where the tears had escaped, before moving her out the door without a single look back.

Detectives Ameno and Maro were racing down the hall, each of them ready to draw their weapons. When Ara didn't show at the station, they came over as fast as they could, afraid they were too late. Lane raised his right arm and tucked her head into her favorite nook in his shoulder. The detectives stopped in front of them as Lane pulled Ara in, giving her the slightest nudge, signaling it was time. That there were more steps to the process, and she had to seal the deal. Walking toward the detectives, she allowed herself to ugly cry, filled with forced gasps for air and full-bodied sobs. She could let it out now, tell them everything.

Maro reached out for Ara and continued to move her down the hall, away from the horrific scene, finally seeing her as a true victim. Ameno put one arm on Lane's back, shook his head with understanding, and reached for his radio pausing until the elevator doors closed, safely taking Ara downstairs and out of the building. Once again, chaos would unfold and forensic teams would funnel inside; no doubt the media would swarm every inch leading up to the taped off hall.

Back at the station, the detectives showed Ara what was on Dr. Dan's video, the piece to the puzzle needed to finally close the case. Raina exiting the front doors of the building the night Brad was murdered, wearing the same oversized dark jacket and hood as the mystery person shown on the security footage. What the detectives didn't know was that Ara already knew she was there.

That night, when she got to the top of the stairs, before opening the door to the corridor, she heard them, Brad and Raina, bickering in hushed voices on the other side. Quiet as a mouse she moved out of sight from the stairwell door window and held her breath. She listened, her heart beating out of her chest, as Raina told him it was now or never before pushing him back and stomping away. Ara carefully opened the door and peered around the corner and watched as Raina stormed to the elevators, Brad following. Even if the security coverage wasn't perfect, she knew somehow she'd be caught on tape. She had even strategically asked Brad to show Raina the gun weeks earlier while they all sipped on wine in their living room. By then, mostly knowing their plan, she needed to make her endgame stronger.

"It scares me to hold it," Ara had lied. "To have that much power in your hands." Taking the bait, Raina had snatched it from Brad, aiming it at the window before passing it back, leaving her prints and saying, "I kinda like it."

Without even knowing, Raina had set herself up to be blamed for Brad's death. Thankfully, Dan had created a second source, capturing her face as she walked away from the scene. That's a narrative Ara would have never thought to create. But it was perfect. Dan held an important piece in her life after all.

Ara listened as Lane detailed their account of what took place in the apartment to the detectives knowing that eventually Raina's partial print would match to the murder weapon, solidifying her guilt.

If only Lane had the courage to talk to her first that New Year's Eve, all of this could have been avoided. *A knight hardly did any good on the rim.* But that was the past, and she was tired of the games. For once she could think about her future.

It turns out, when push comes to shove, one night could change it all. A single moment forcing its players into corners unplanned for. Brad was right when he said chess was a lot like life. But in life, you should never doubt a queen. Even in a concerted effort for deliberate sacrifice, her power can be limitless. And this time, she won her game.

ABOUT THE AUTHOR

Caitlin Sara works in digital marketing, but writing fiction has always been her passion. *Rooked* is her debut thriller. Born and raised in New Jersey, she is currently working on her second novel of the same genre.

caitlinsara.com   @CSaraBooks

Made in the USA
San Bernardino, CA
06 December 2019